WAŁUK

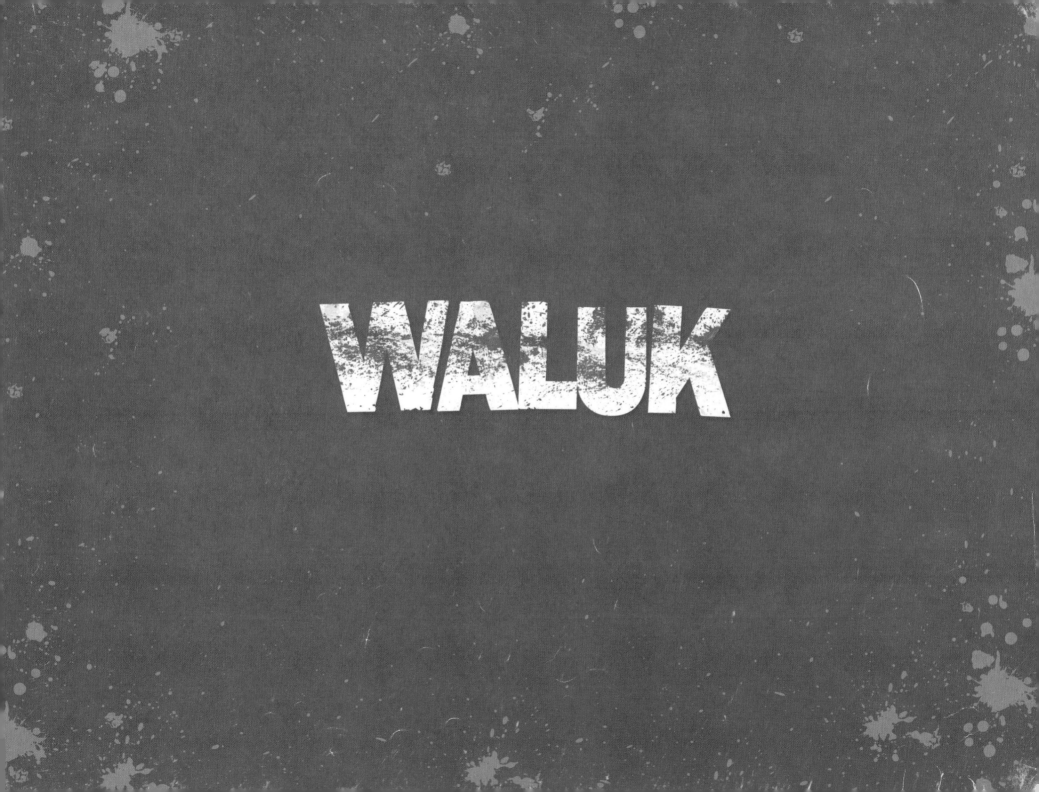

Story by Emilio Ruiz
Illustrated by Ana Miralles
Translation and adapted by Dan Oliverio

First American edition published in 2013 by Graphic Universe™.

Graphic Universe™
A division of Lerner Publishing Group, Inc.
241 First Avenue North
Minneapolis, MN 55401 U.S.A.

Website address: www.lernerbooks.com

Library of Congress Cataloging-in-Publication Data

Ruiz, Emilio.
    [Wáluk. English.]
    Waluk / by Emilio Ruiz ; illustrated by Ana Miralles ; translated and adapted by Dan Oliverio.
        p.   cm.
    Originally published in Spanish in Bilbao, Spain, by Astiberri, in 2011, under the title: Wáluk.
    Summary: Waluk, a young polar bear abandoned by his mother, learns how to fend for himself with the help of Manitok, a cranky old bear who teaches Waluk about seals, foxes, changing seasons, and human beings. End notes discuss animal habitats and environmental issues.
    ISBN 978-1-4677-1598-0 (lib. bdg. : alk. paper)
    ISBN 978-1-4677-2057-1 (eBook)
    1. Graphic novels. [1. Graphic novels. 2. Polar bear–Fiction. 3. Bears–Fiction.
4. Tundras–Fiction.] I. Miralles, 1959– illustrator. II. Oliverio, Dan. III. Title.
PZ7.7.R85Wal 2013
741.5′946–dc23   2012047787

Manufactured in the United States of America
1 – CG – 7/15/13

WALUK

STORY BY **EMILIO RUIZ** ILLUSTRATED BY **ANA MIRALLES**
TRANSLATED AND ADAPTED BY **DAN OLIVERIO**

GRAPHIC UNIVERSE™ • MINNEAPOLIS

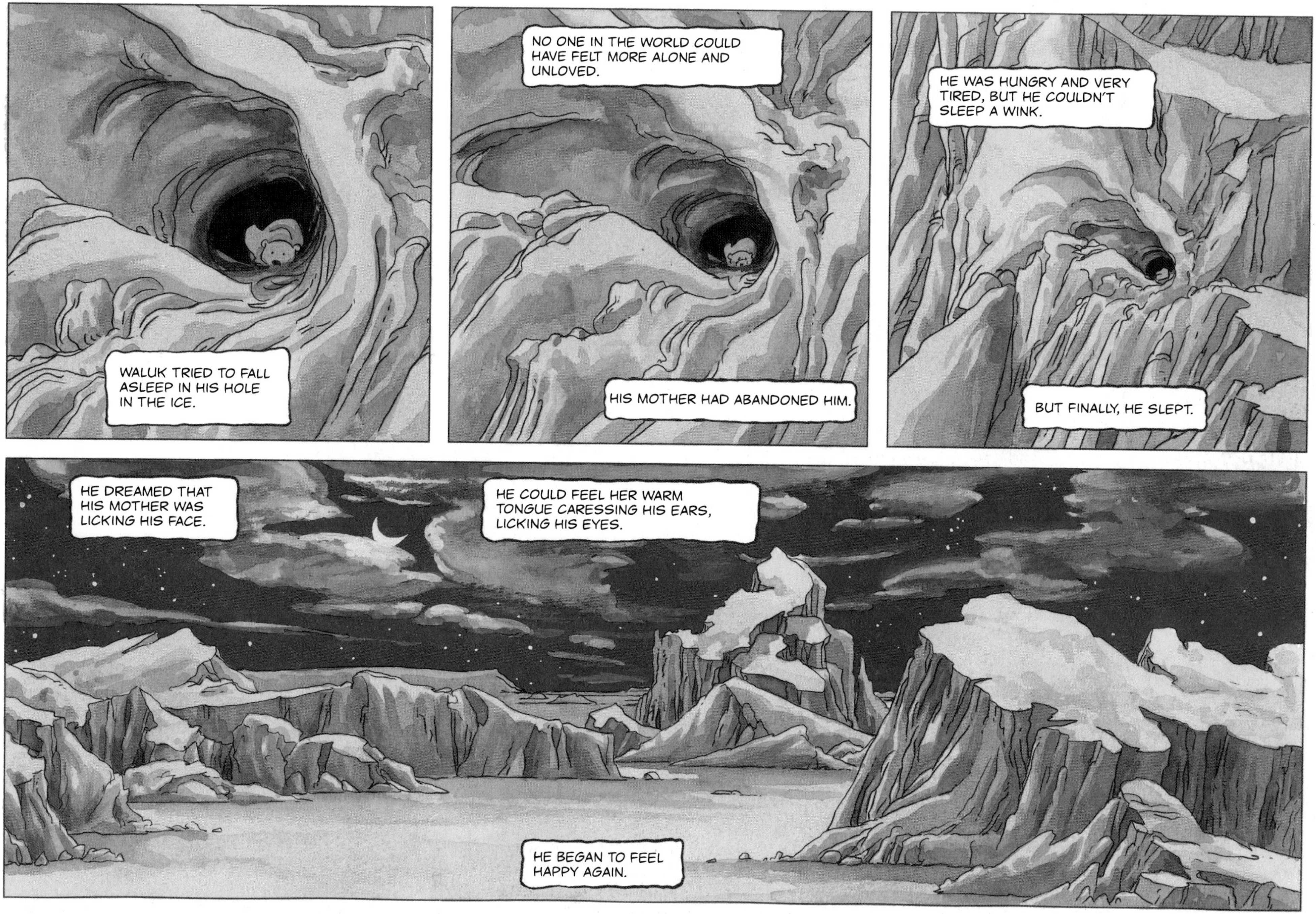
WALUK TRIED TO FALL ASLEEP IN HIS HOLE IN THE ICE.
NO ONE IN THE WORLD COULD HAVE FELT MORE ALONE AND UNLOVED.
HIS MOTHER HAD ABANDONED HIM.
HE WAS HUNGRY AND VERY TIRED, BUT HE COULDN'T SLEEP A WINK.
BUT FINALLY, HE SLEPT.
HE DREAMED THAT HIS MOTHER WAS LICKING HIS FACE.
HE COULD FEEL HER WARM TONGUE CARESSING HIS EARS, LICKING HIS EYES.
HE BEGAN TO FEEL HAPPY AGAIN.

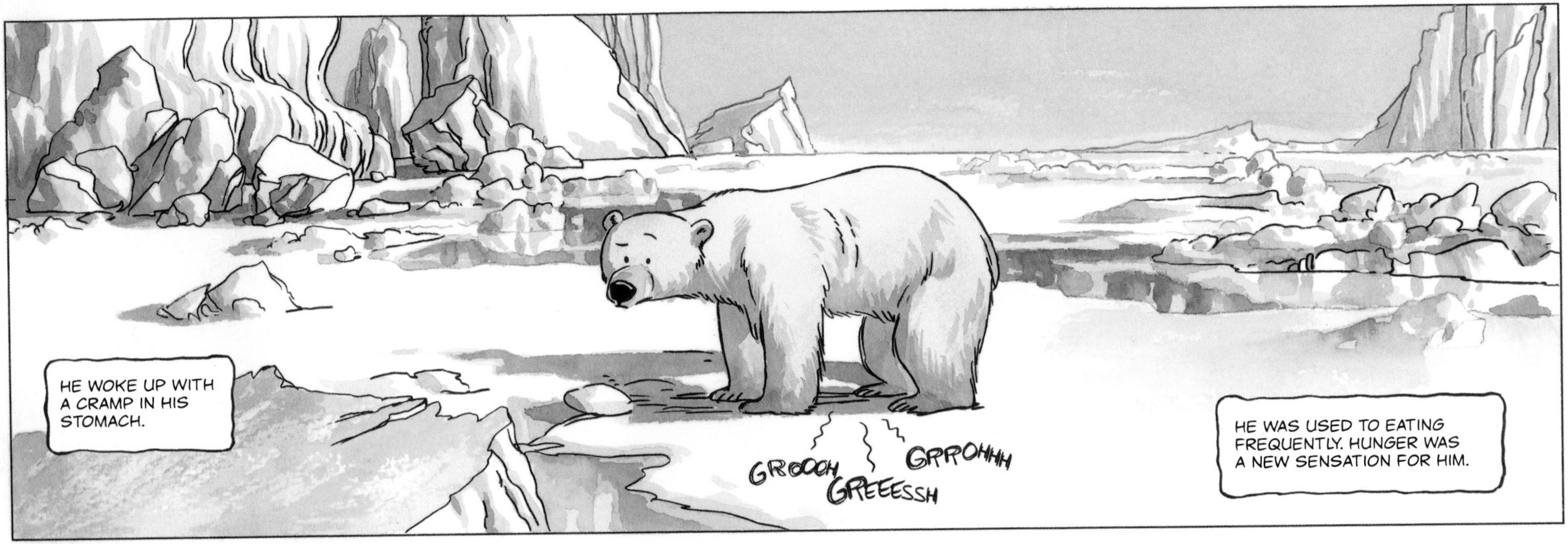
HE WOKE UP WITH A CRAMP IN HIS STOMACH.
GROOOH
GREEESSH
GRROHHH
HE WAS USED TO EATING FREQUENTLY. HUNGER WAS A NEW SENSATION FOR HIM.

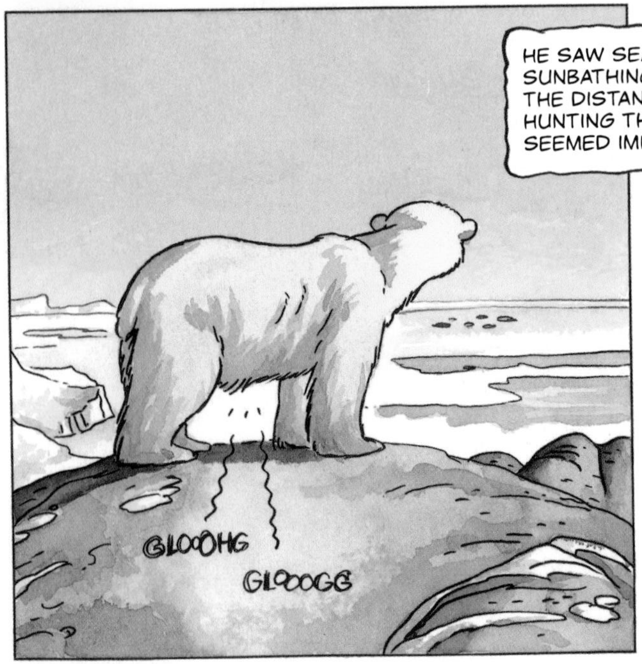
HE SAW SEALS SUNBATHING IN THE DISTANCE, BUT HUNTING THEM SEEMED IMPOSSIBLE.
GLOOOHG
GLOOOGG

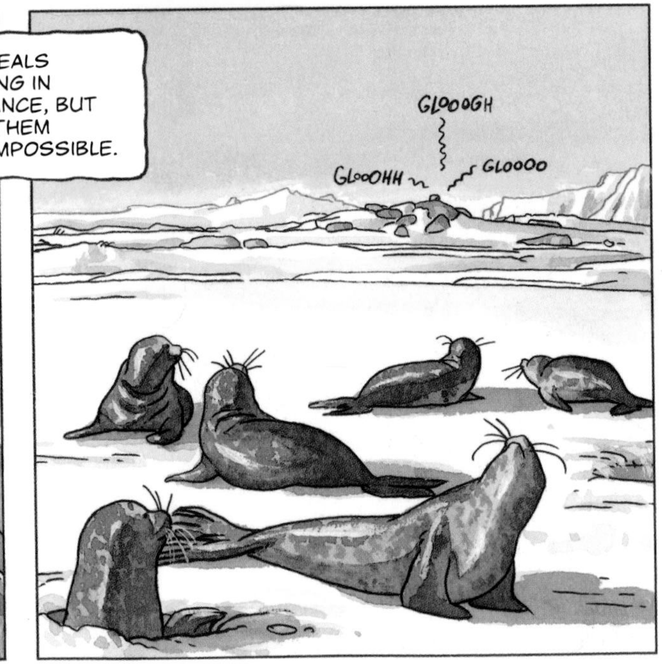
GLOOOGH
GLOOHH
GLOOOO

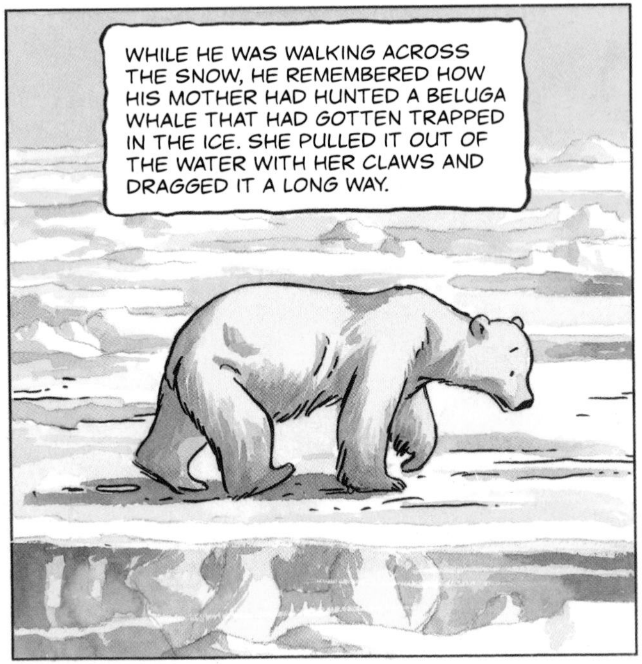
WHILE HE WAS WALKING ACROSS THE SNOW, HE REMEMBERED HOW HIS MOTHER HAD HUNTED A BELUGA WHALE THAT HAD GOTTEN TRAPPED IN THE ICE. SHE PULLED IT OUT OF THE WATER WITH HER CLAWS AND DRAGGED IT A LONG WAY.

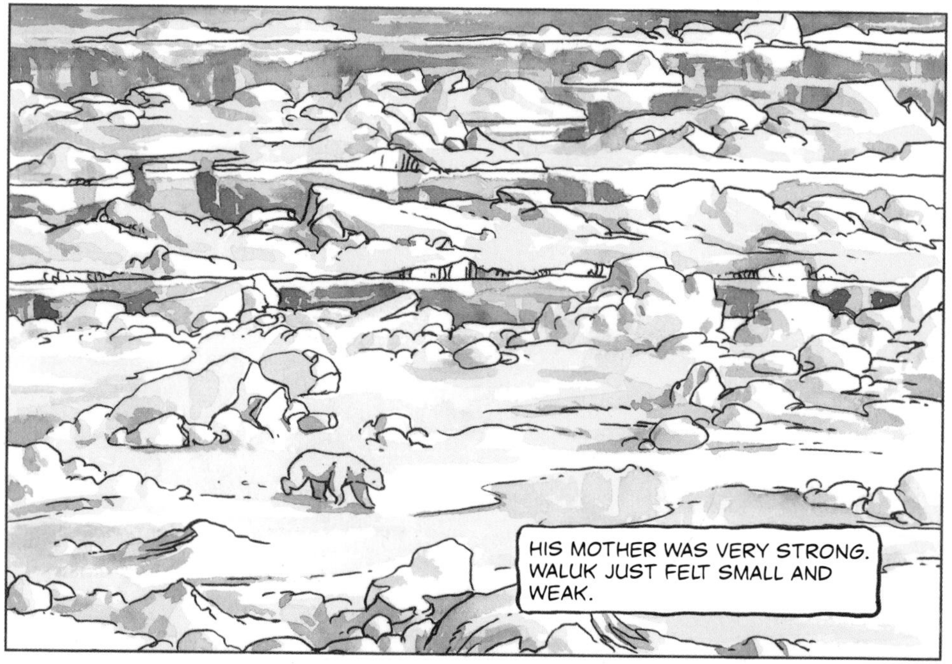
HIS MOTHER WAS VERY STRONG. WALUK JUST FELT SMALL AND WEAK.

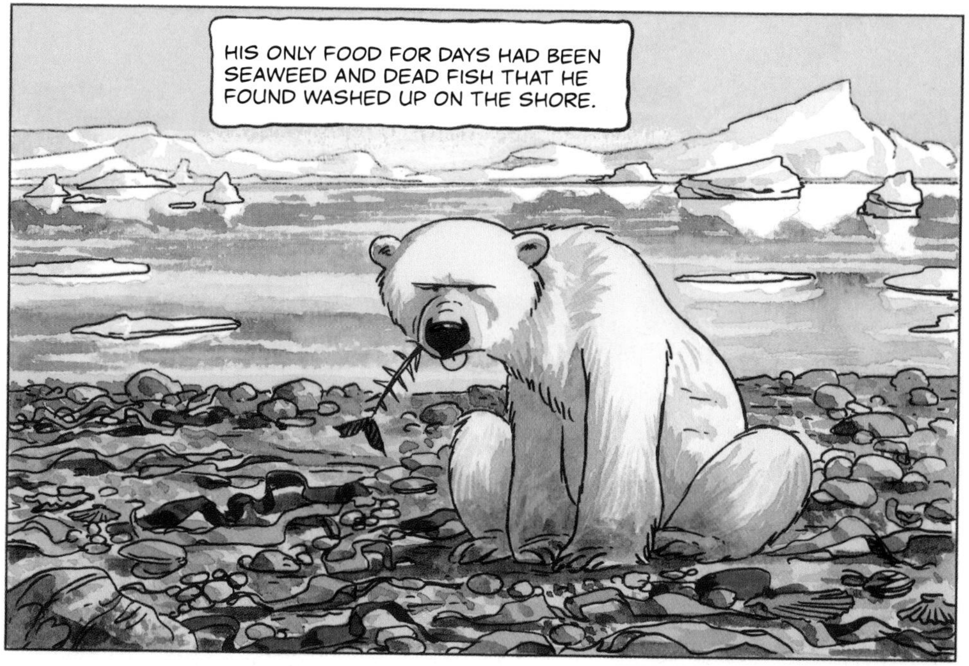
HIS ONLY FOOD FOR DAYS HAD BEEN SEAWEED AND DEAD FISH THAT HE FOUND WASHED UP ON THE SHORE.

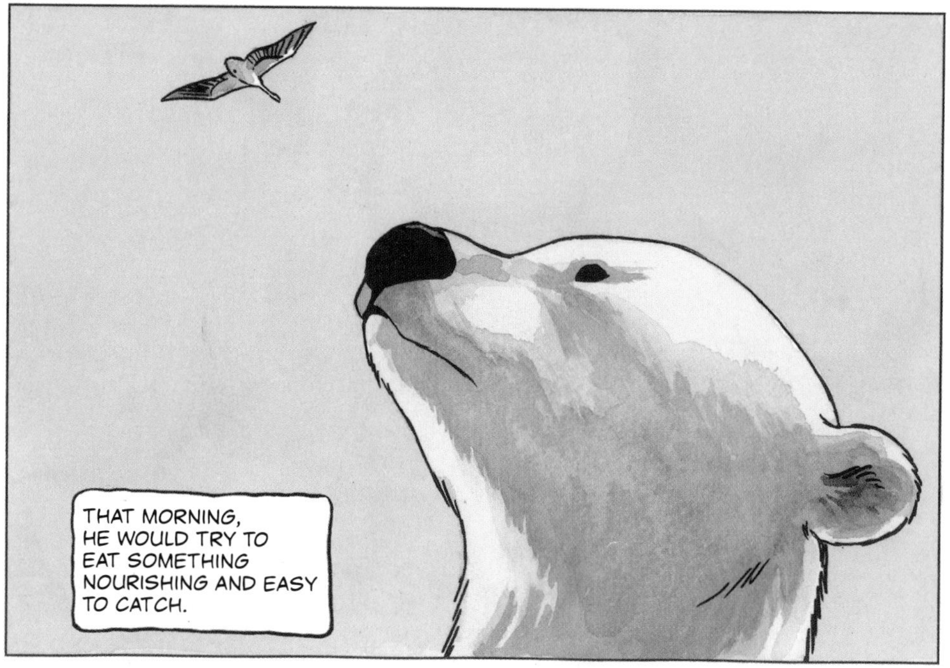
THAT MORNING, HE WOULD TRY TO EAT SOMETHING NOURISHING AND EASY TO CATCH.

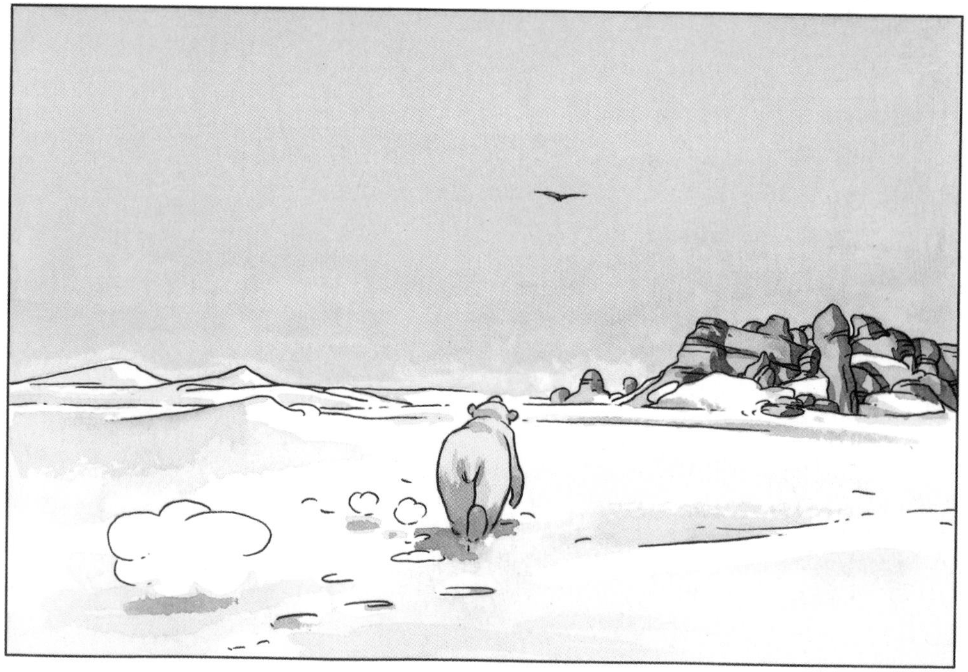

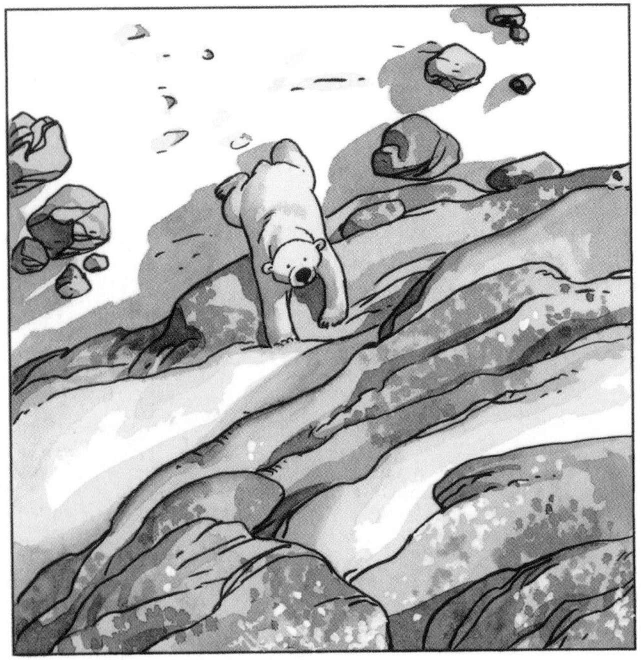
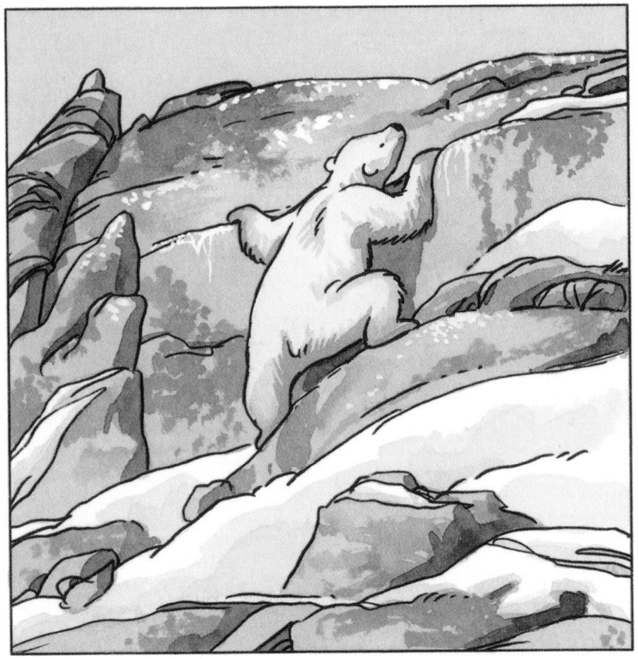
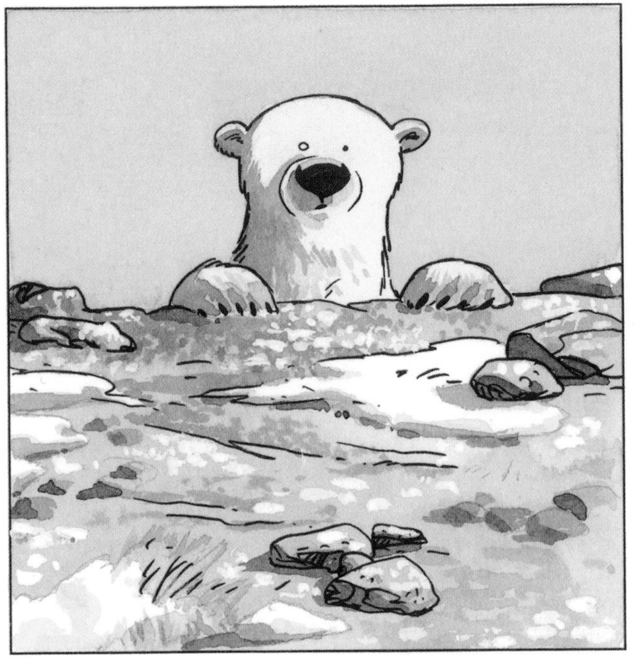
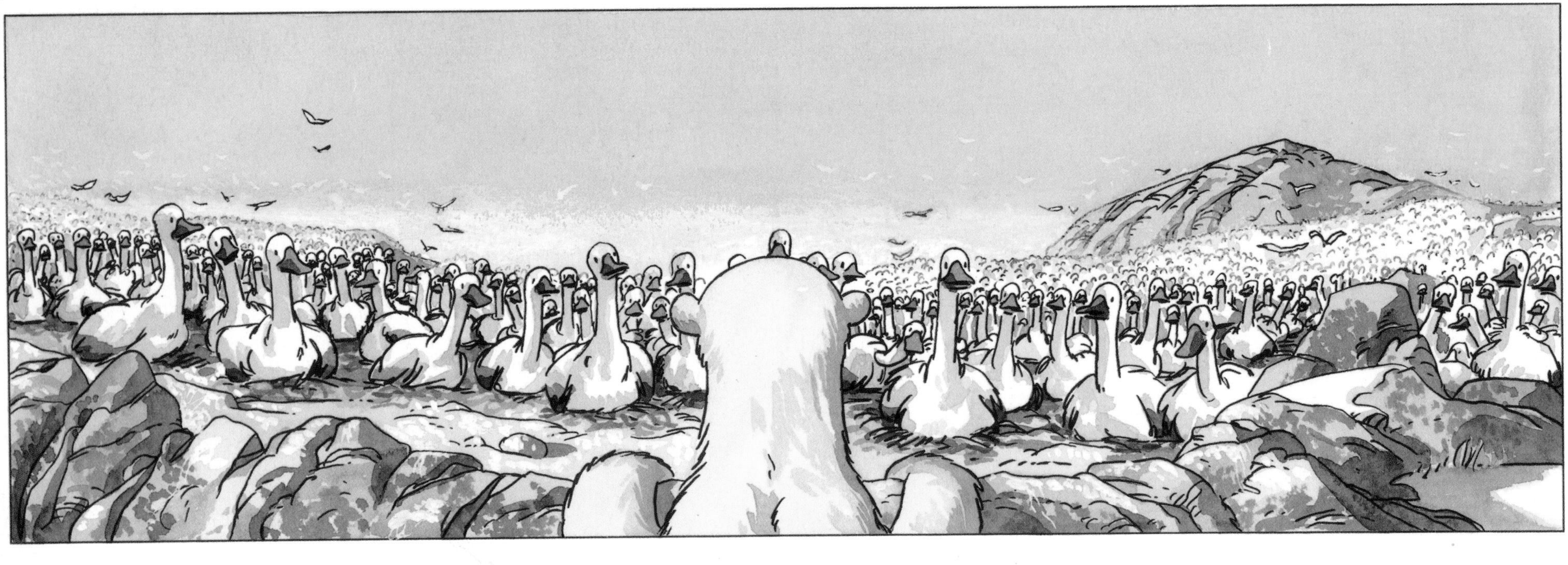

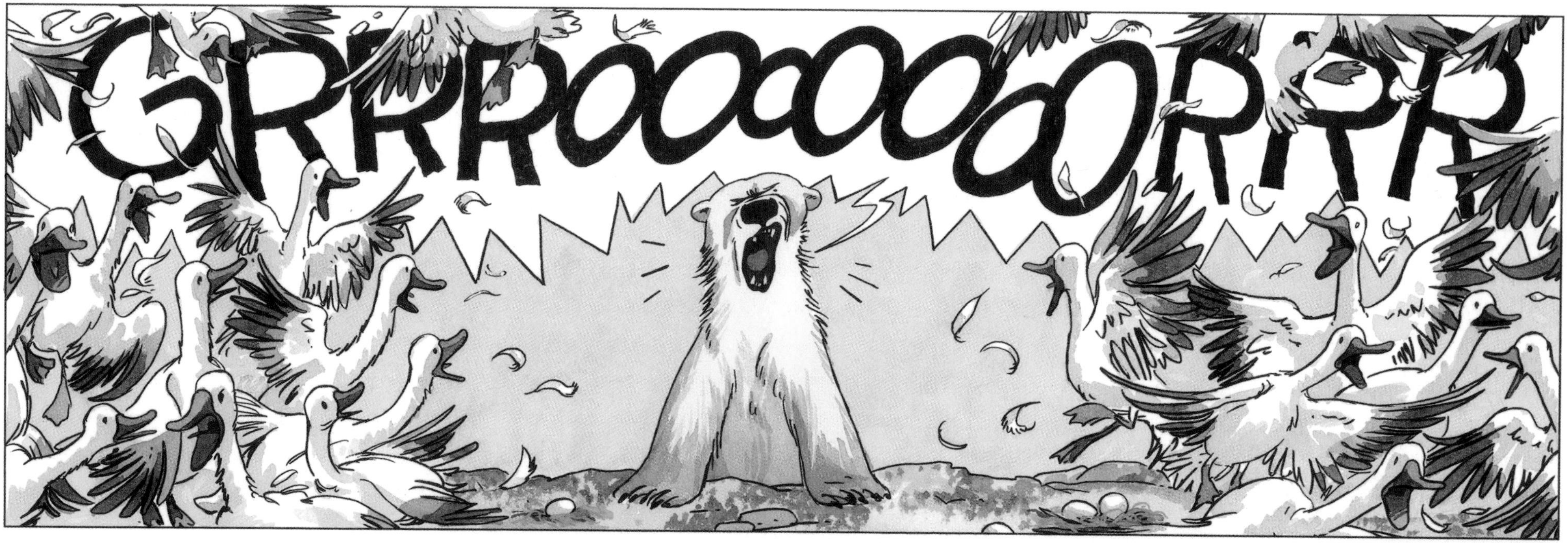
GRRROOOOOOORRRR

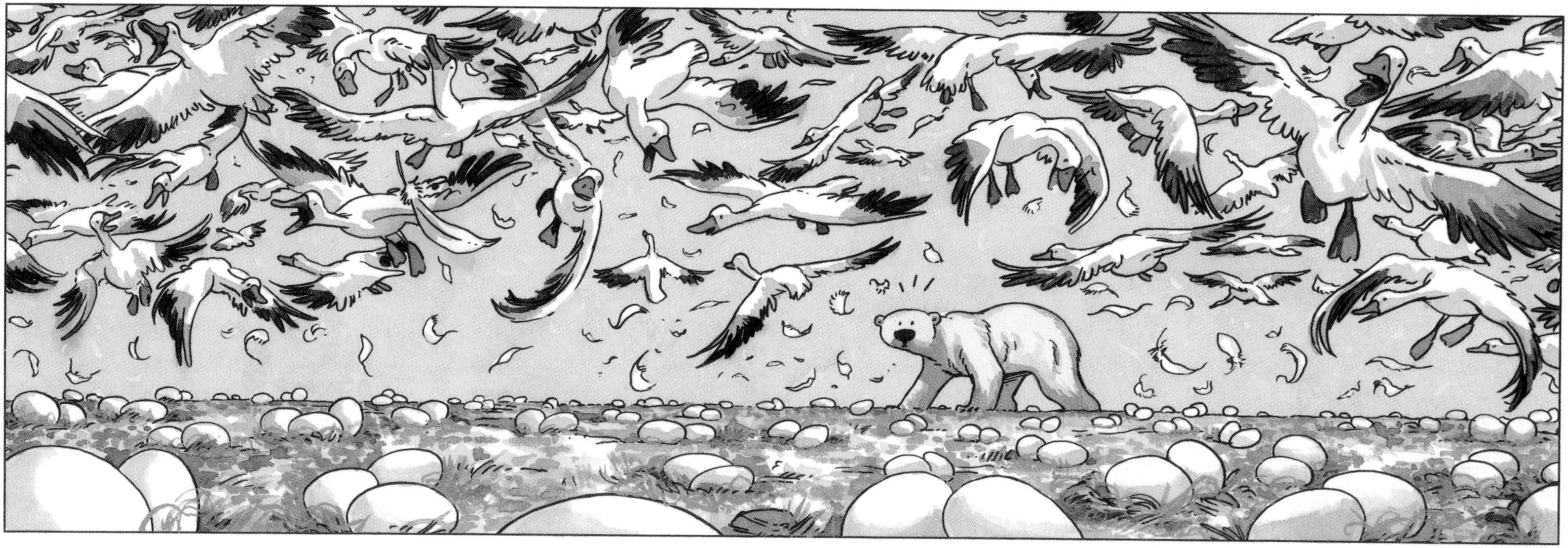

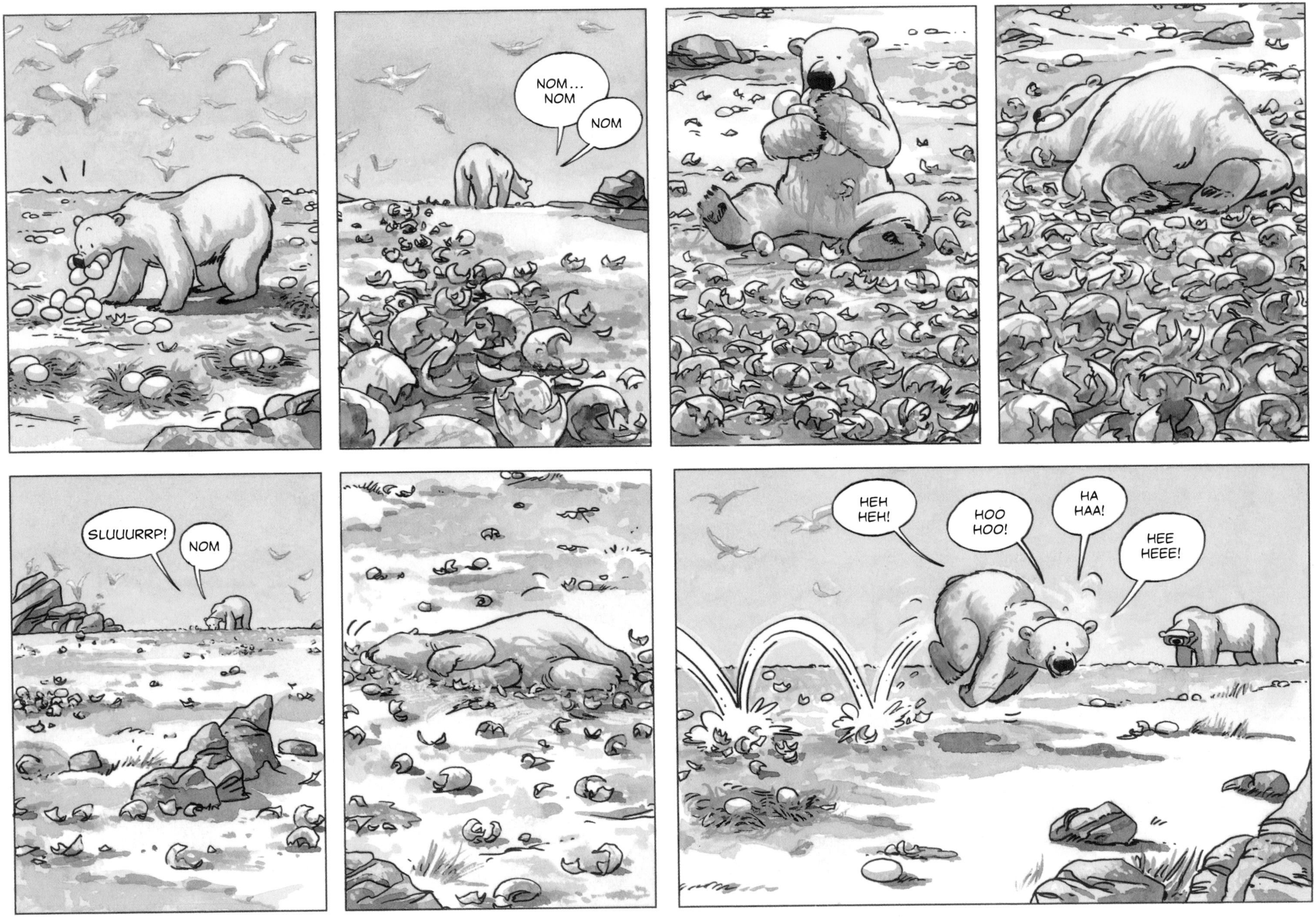
NOM... NOM
NOM
SLUUURRP!
NOM
HEH HEH!
HOO HOO!
HA HAA!
HEE HEEE!

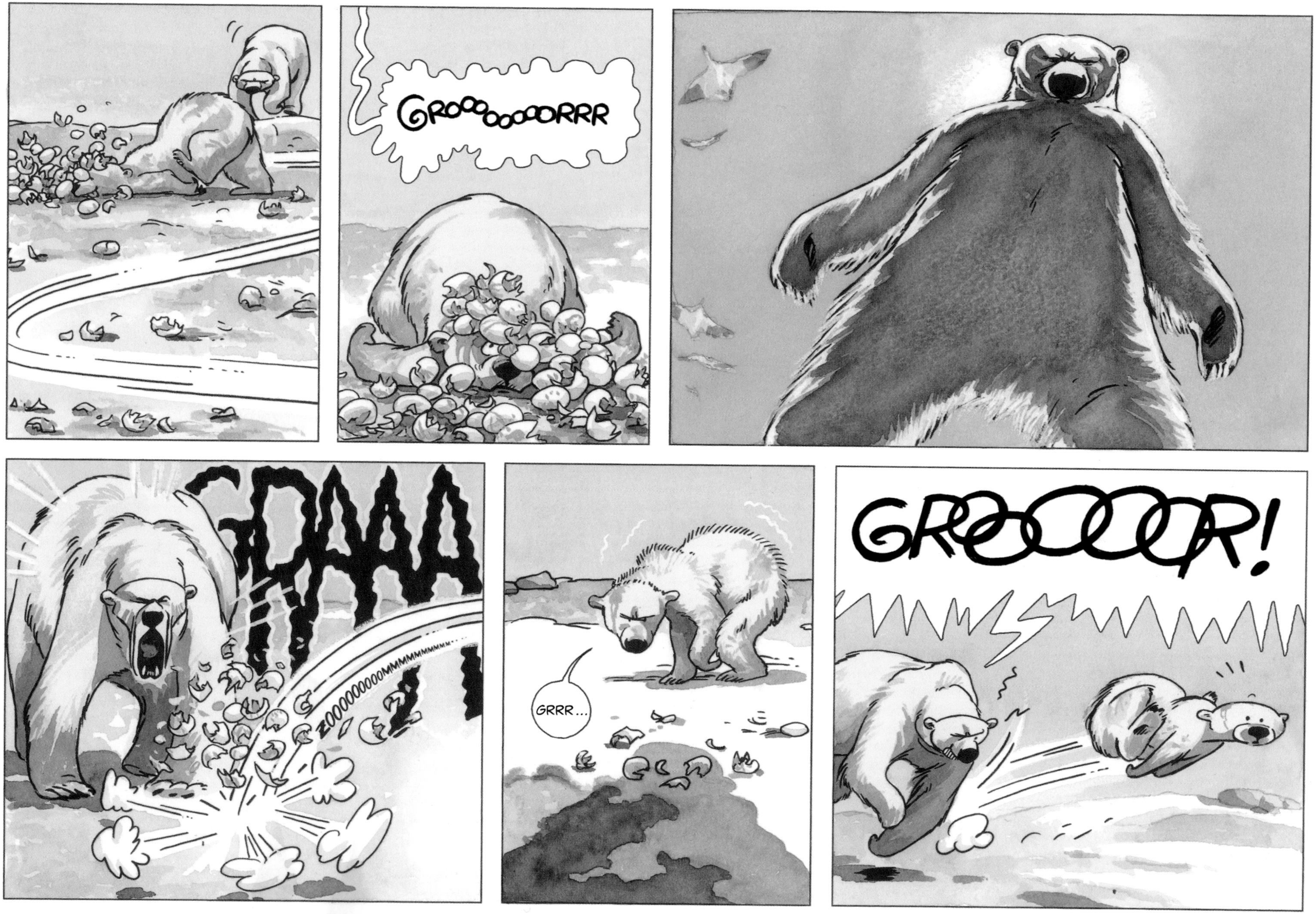
GROOOOOOOORRR
ZOOOOOOOOOOOMMMMMMMMMMM...
GRRR...
GROOOOR!

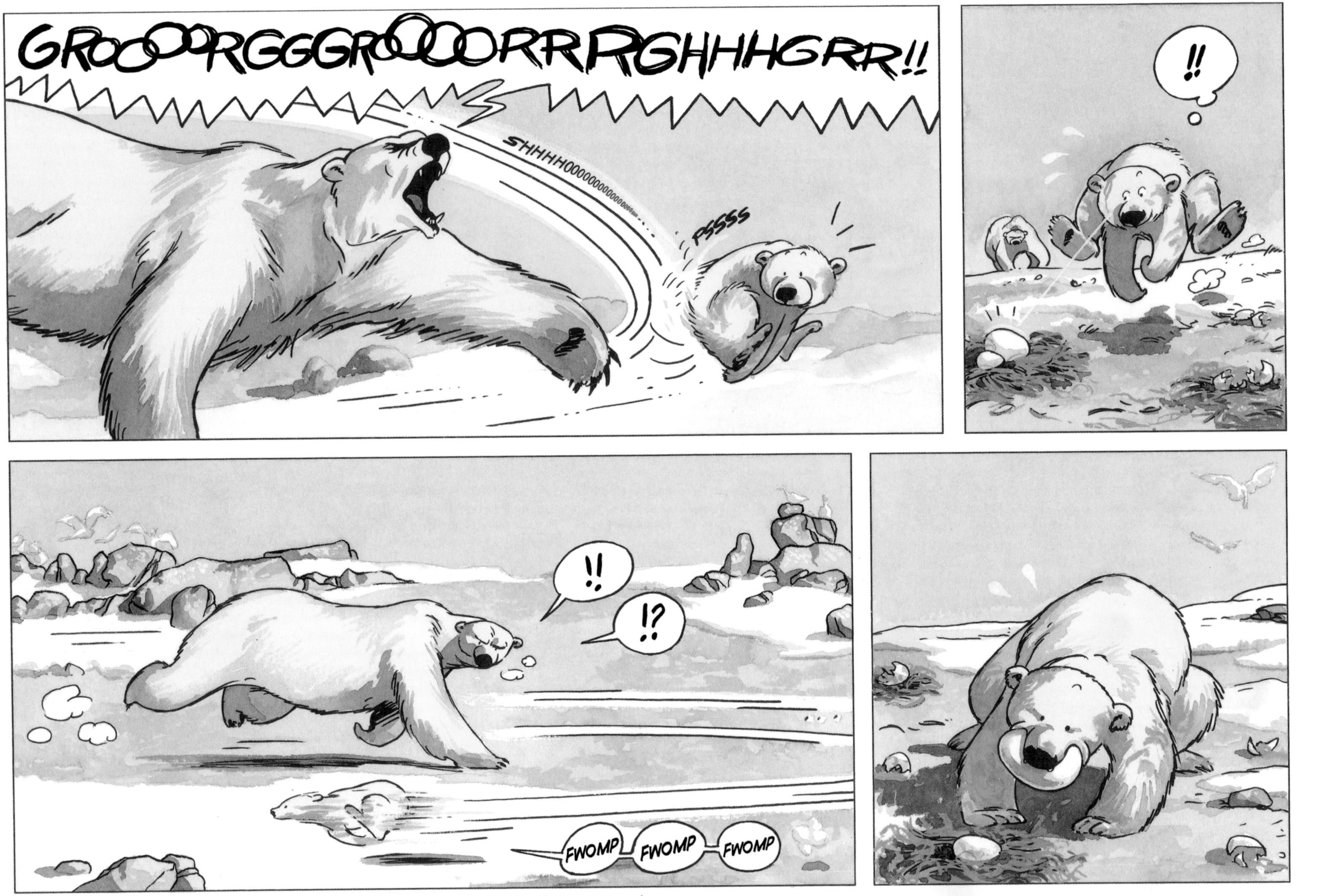
GROOOORGGGROOOOORRRRGHHHGRR!!
SHHHHOOOOOOOOOOOOOOOOOOO...
PSSSS
!!
!!
!?
FWOMP
FWOMP
FWOMP

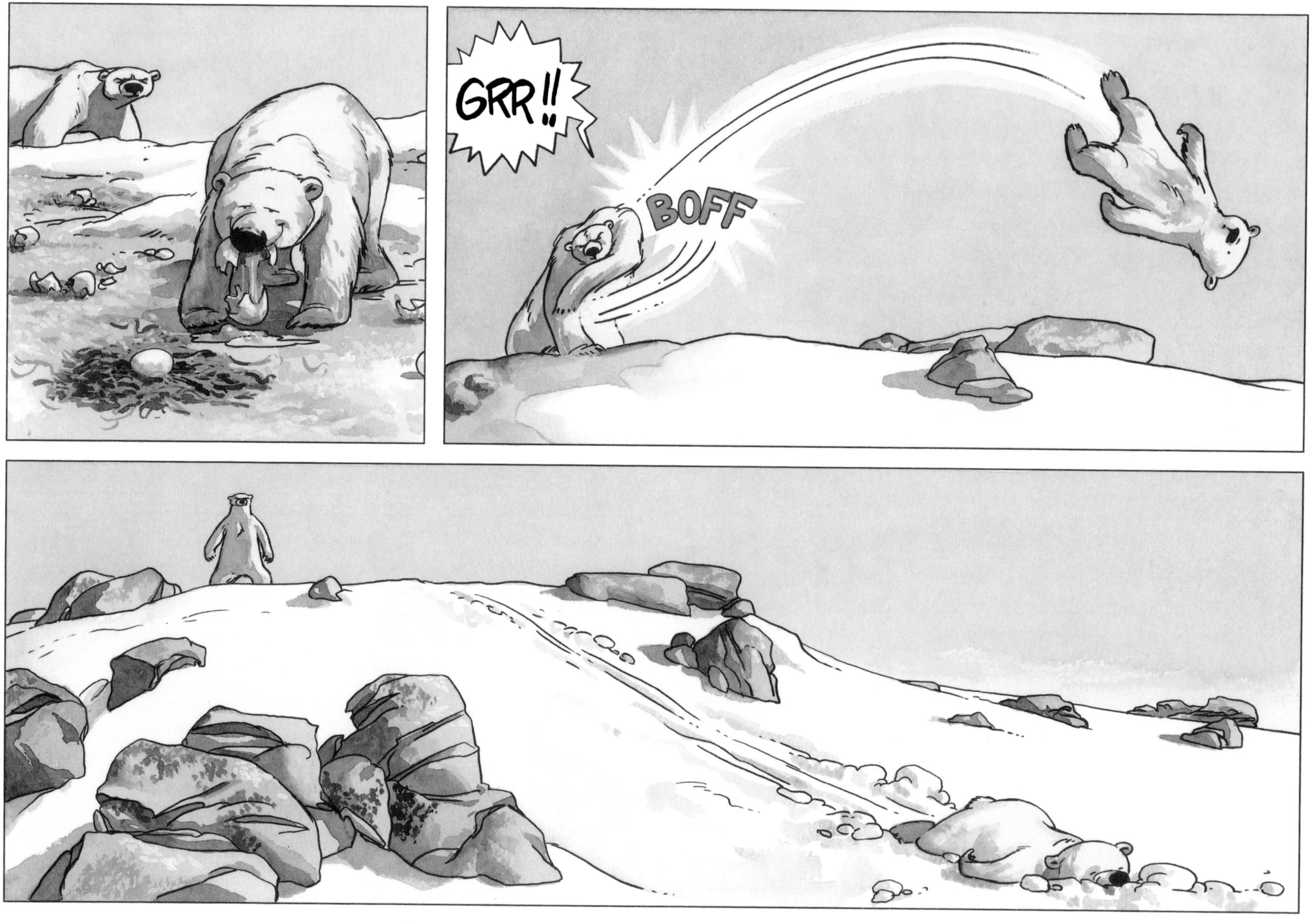
GRR!!
BOFF

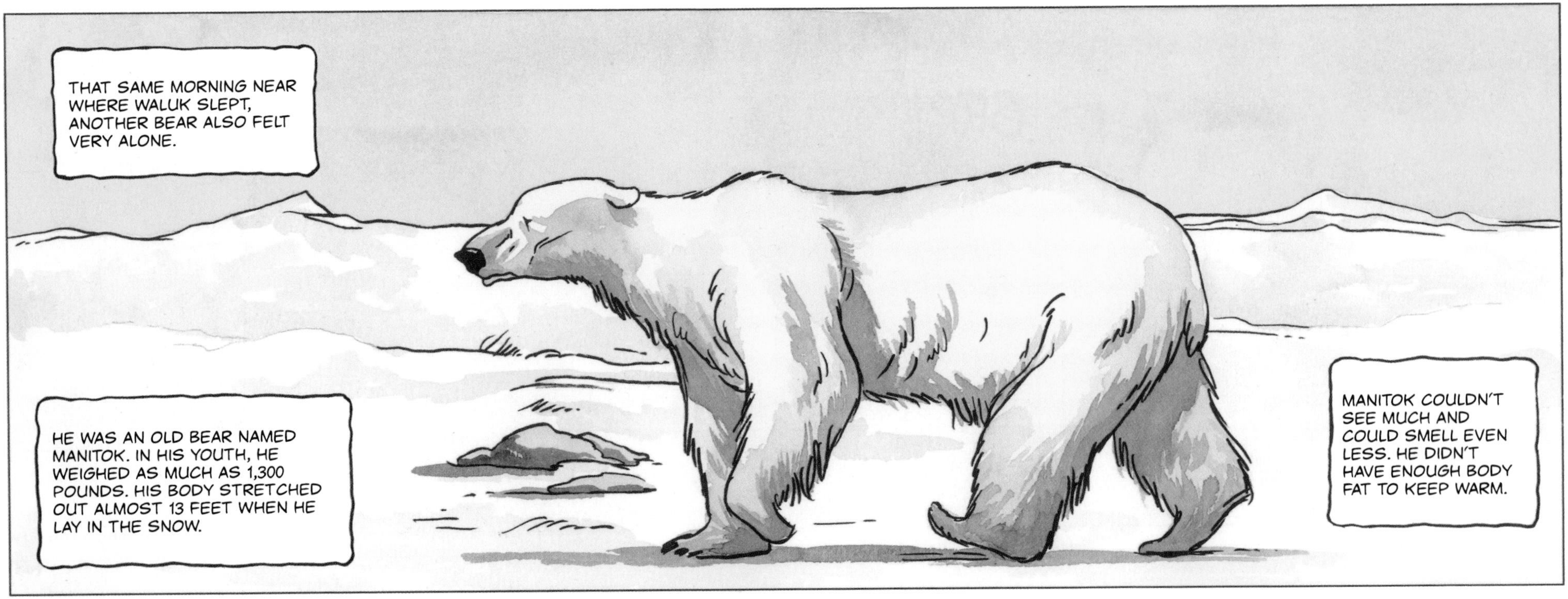
THAT SAME MORNING NEAR WHERE WALUK SLEPT, ANOTHER BEAR ALSO FELT VERY ALONE.
HE WAS AN OLD BEAR NAMED MANITOK. IN HIS YOUTH, HE WEIGHED AS MUCH AS 1,300 POUNDS. HIS BODY STRETCHED OUT ALMOST 13 FEET WHEN HE LAY IN THE SNOW.
MANITOK COULDN'T SEE MUCH AND COULD SMELL EVEN LESS. HE DIDN'T HAVE ENOUGH BODY FAT TO KEEP WARM.

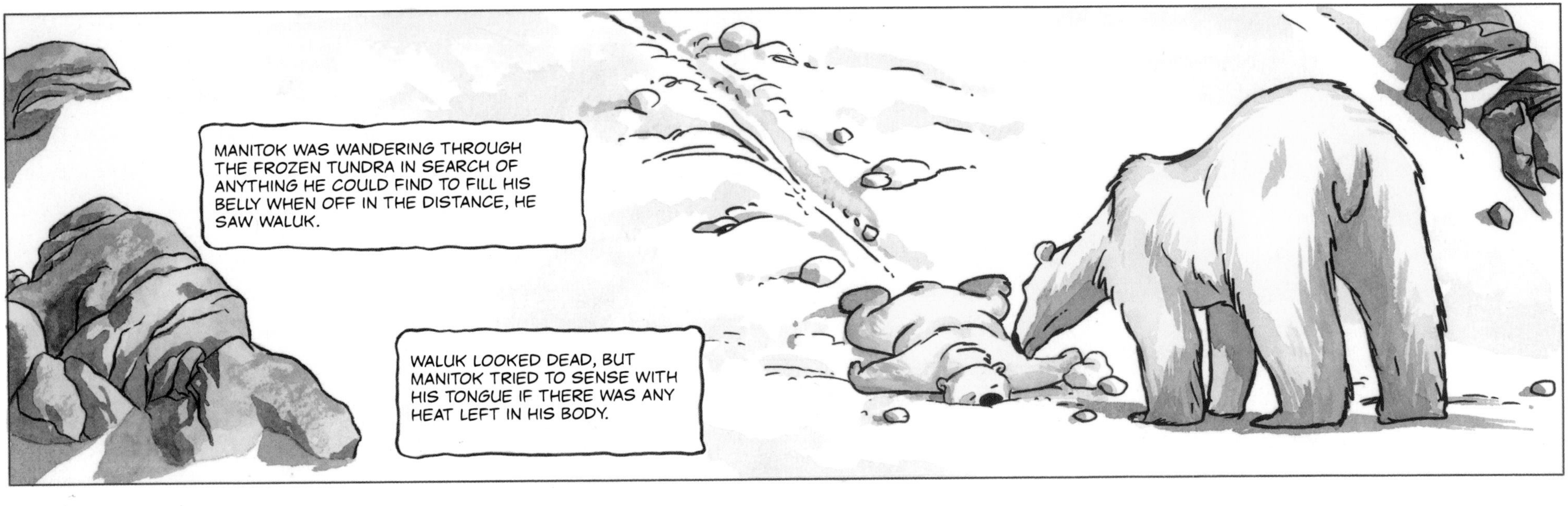
MANITOK WAS WANDERING THROUGH THE FROZEN TUNDRA IN SEARCH OF ANYTHING HE COULD FIND TO FILL HIS BELLY WHEN OFF IN THE DISTANCE, HE SAW WALUK.
WALUK LOOKED DEAD, BUT MANITOK TRIED TO SENSE WITH HIS TONGUE IF THERE WAS ANY HEAT LEFT IN HIS BODY.

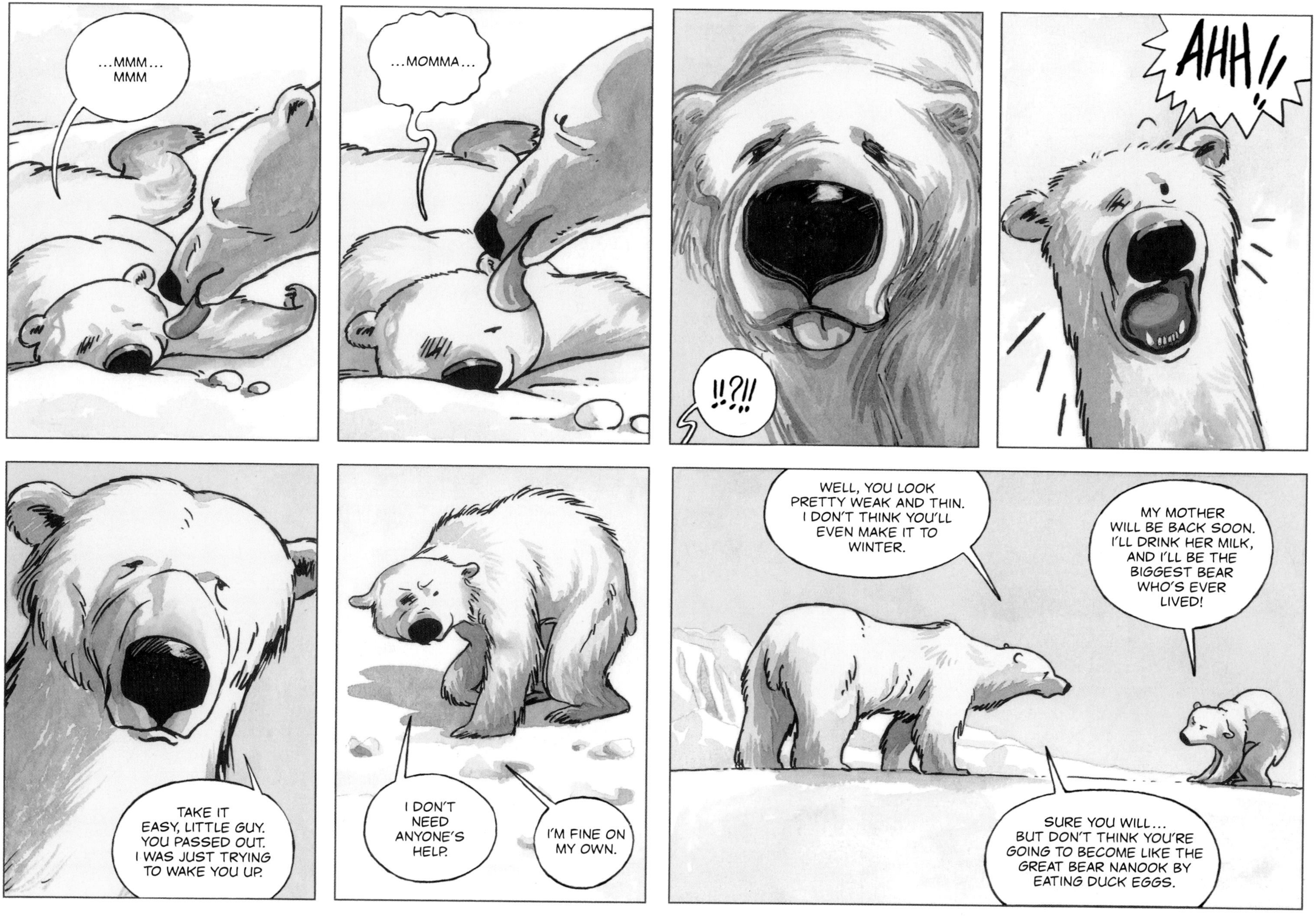
...MMM... MMM
...MOMMA...
!!?!!
AHH!!
TAKE IT EASY, LITTLE GUY. YOU PASSED OUT. I WAS JUST TRYING TO WAKE YOU UP.
I DON'T NEED ANYONE'S HELP.
I'M FINE ON MY OWN.
WELL, YOU LOOK PRETTY WEAK AND THIN. I DON'T THINK YOU'LL EVEN MAKE IT TO WINTER.
MY MOTHER WILL BE BACK SOON. I'LL DRINK HER MILK, AND I'LL BE THE BIGGEST BEAR WHO'S EVER LIVED!
SURE YOU WILL... BUT DON'T THINK YOU'RE GOING TO BECOME LIKE THE GREAT BEAR NANOOK BY EATING DUCK EGGS.

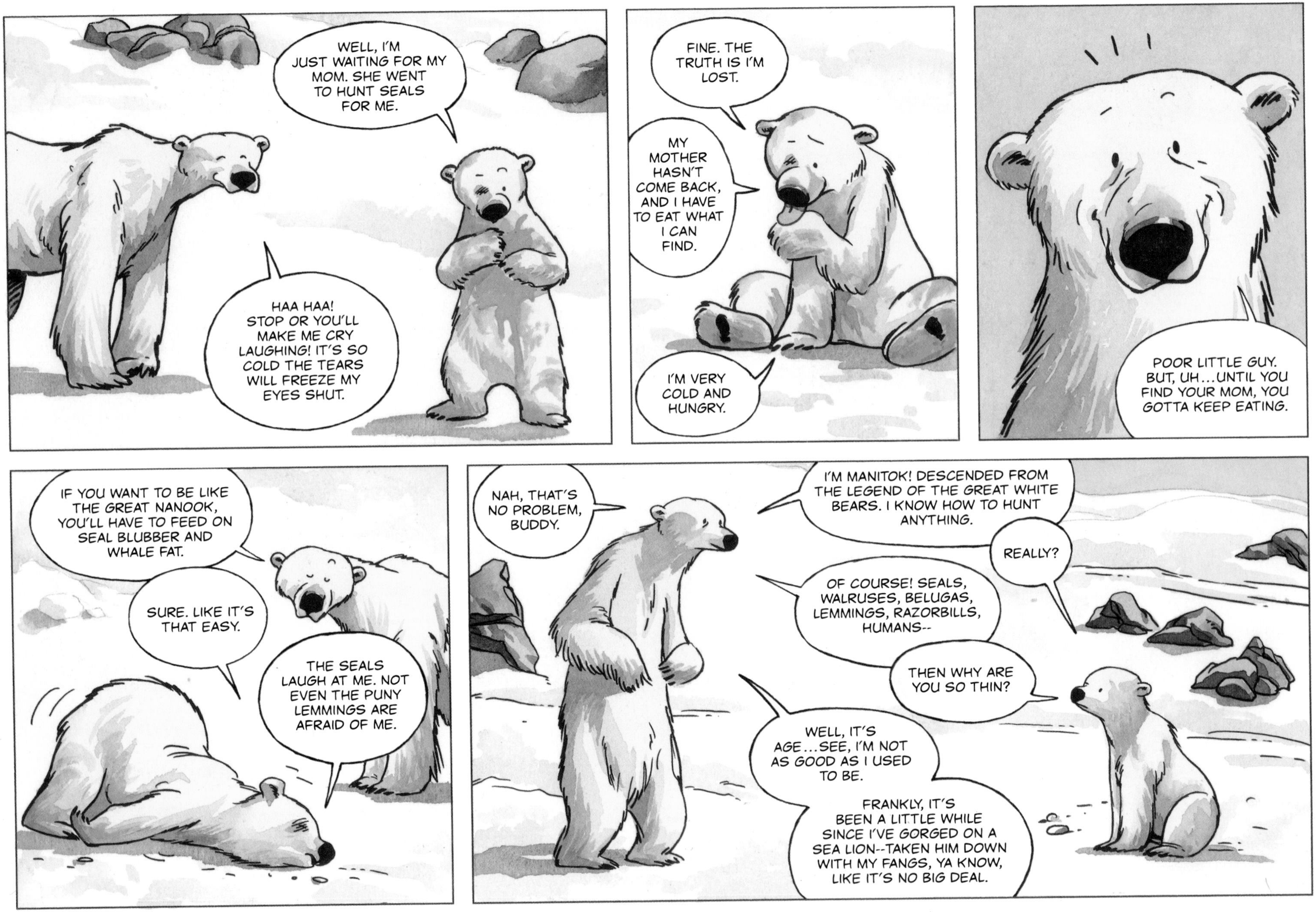

WELL, I'M JUST WAITING FOR MY MOM. SHE WENT TO HUNT SEALS FOR ME.
HAA HAA! STOP OR YOU'LL MAKE ME CRY LAUGHING! IT'S SO COLD THE TEARS WILL FREEZE MY EYES SHUT.
FINE. THE TRUTH IS I'M LOST.
MY MOTHER HASN'T COME BACK, AND I HAVE TO EAT WHAT I CAN FIND.
I'M VERY COLD AND HUNGRY.
POOR LITTLE GUY. BUT, UH...UNTIL YOU FIND YOUR MOM, YOU GOTTA KEEP EATING.
IF YOU WANT TO BE LIKE THE GREAT NANOOK, YOU'LL HAVE TO FEED ON SEAL BLUBBER AND WHALE FAT.
SURE. LIKE IT'S THAT EASY.
THE SEALS LAUGH AT ME. NOT EVEN THE PUNY LEMMINGS ARE AFRAID OF ME.
NAH, THAT'S NO PROBLEM, BUDDY.
I'M MANITOK! DESCENDED FROM THE LEGEND OF THE GREAT WHITE BEARS. I KNOW HOW TO HUNT ANYTHING.
REALLY?
OF COURSE! SEALS, WALRUSES, BELUGAS, LEMMINGS, RAZORBILLS, HUMANS--
THEN WHY ARE YOU SO THIN?
WELL, IT'S AGE...SEE, I'M NOT AS GOOD AS I USED TO BE.
FRANKLY, IT'S BEEN A LITTLE WHILE SINCE I'VE GORGED ON A SEA LION--TAKEN HIM DOWN WITH MY FANGS, YA KNOW, LIKE IT'S NO BIG DEAL.

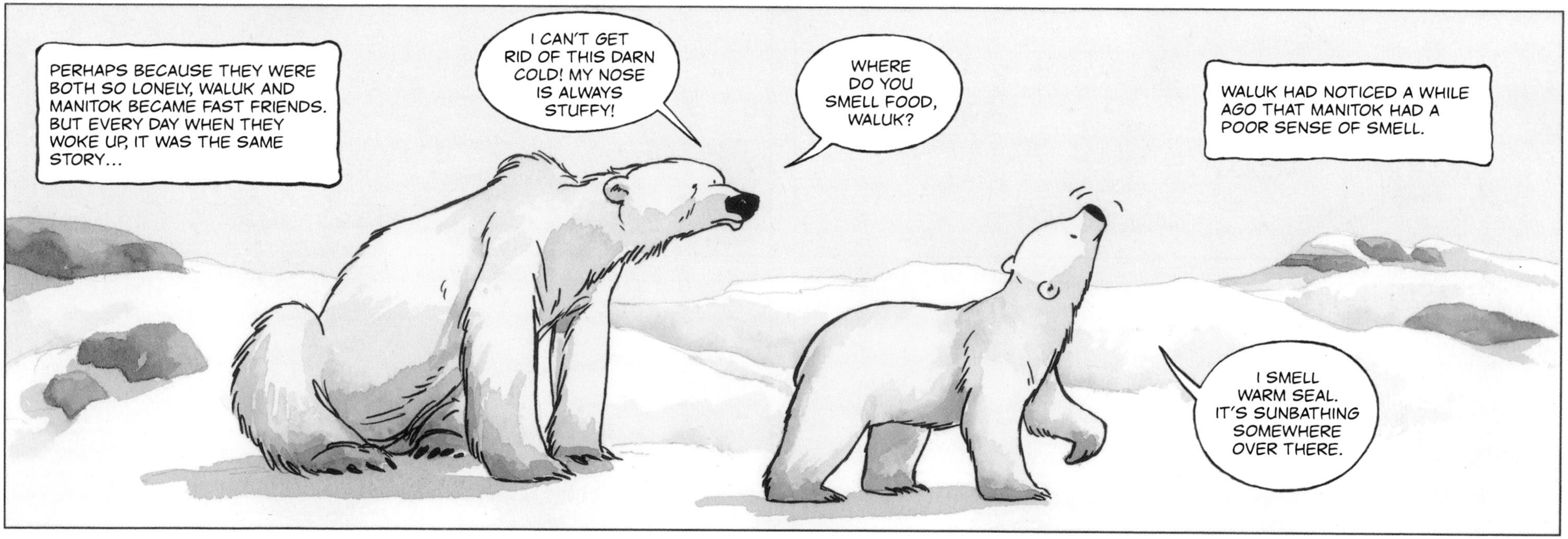
PERHAPS BECAUSE THEY WERE BOTH SO LONELY, WALUK AND MANITOK BECAME FAST FRIENDS. BUT EVERY DAY WHEN THEY WOKE UP, IT WAS THE SAME STORY...
I CAN'T GET RID OF THIS DARN COLD! MY NOSE IS ALWAYS STUFFY!
WHERE DO YOU SMELL FOOD, WALUK?
WALUK HAD NOTICED A WHILE AGO THAT MANITOK HAD A POOR SENSE OF SMELL.
I SMELL WARM SEAL. IT'S SUNBATHING SOMEWHERE OVER THERE.

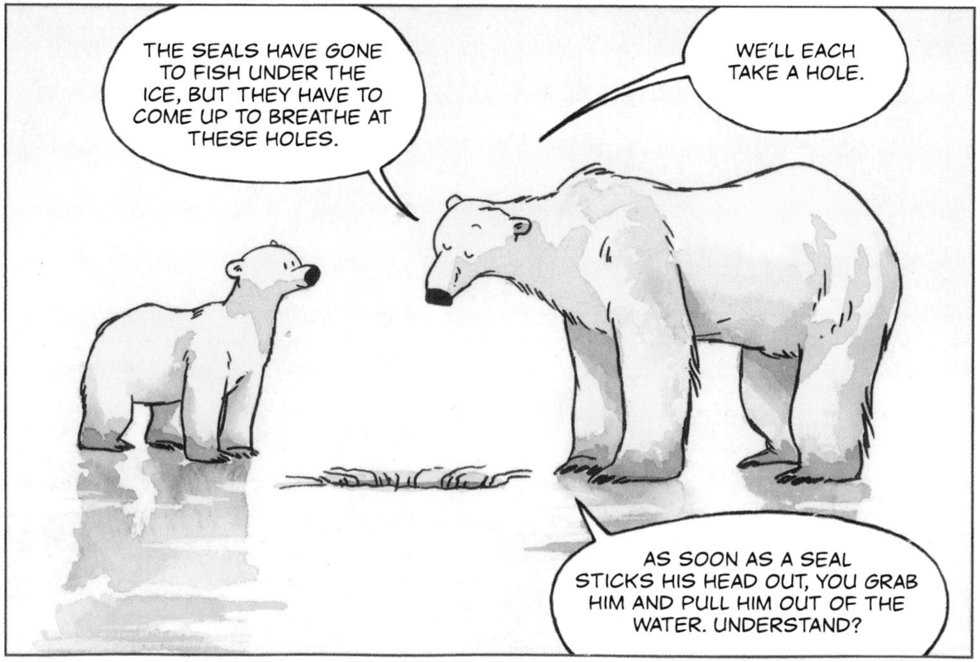
THE SEALS HAVE GONE TO FISH UNDER THE ICE, BUT THEY HAVE TO COME UP TO BREATHE AT THESE HOLES.
WE'LL EACH TAKE A HOLE.
AS SOON AS A SEAL STICKS HIS HEAD OUT, YOU GRAB HIM AND PULL HIM OUT OF THE WATER. UNDERSTAND?

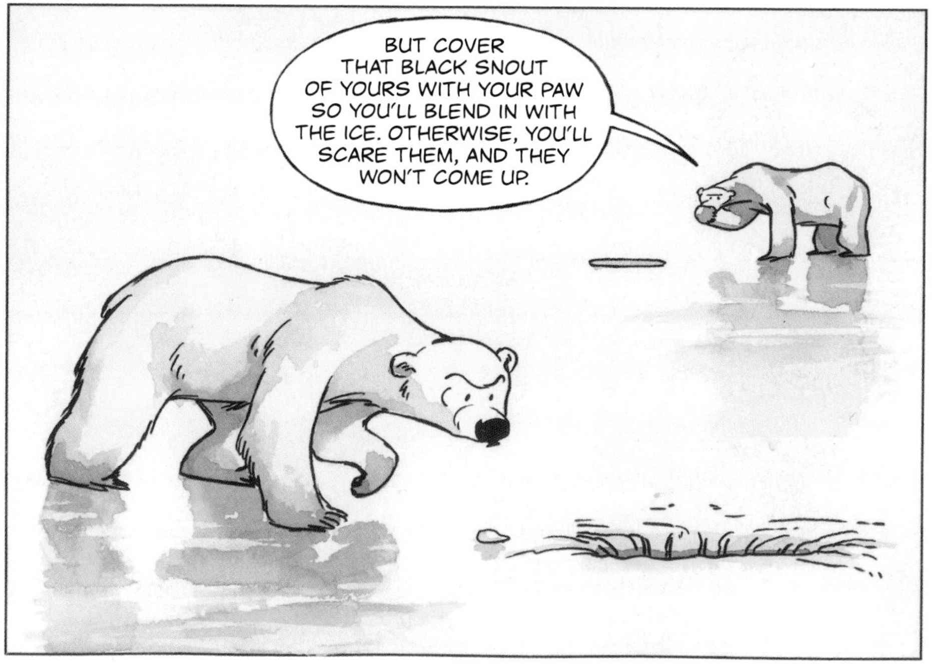
BUT COVER THAT BLACK SNOUT OF YOURS WITH YOUR PAW SO YOU'LL BLEND IN WITH THE ICE. OTHERWISE, YOU'LL SCARE THEM, AND THEY WON'T COME UP.

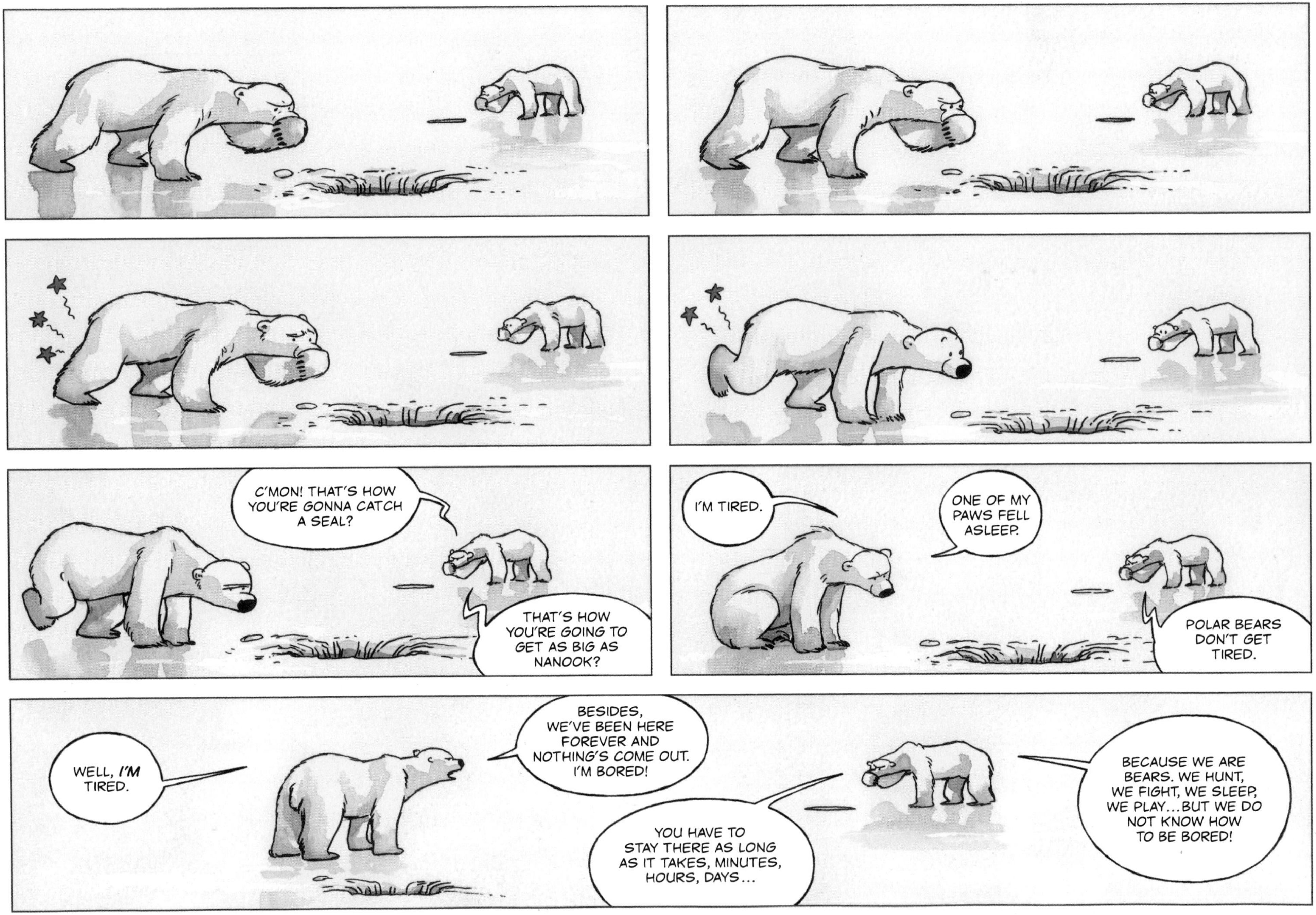
C'MON! THAT'S HOW YOU'RE GONNA CATCH A SEAL?
THAT'S HOW YOU'RE GOING TO GET AS BIG AS NANOOK?
I'M TIRED.
ONE OF MY PAWS FELL ASLEEP.
POLAR BEARS DON'T GET TIRED.
WELL, ***I'M*** TIRED.
BESIDES, WE'VE BEEN HERE FOREVER AND NOTHING'S COME OUT. I'M BORED!
YOU HAVE TO STAY THERE AS LONG AS IT TAKES, MINUTES, HOURS, DAYS...
BECAUSE WE ARE BEARS. WE HUNT, WE FIGHT, WE SLEEP, WE PLAY...BUT WE DO NOT KNOW HOW TO BE BORED!

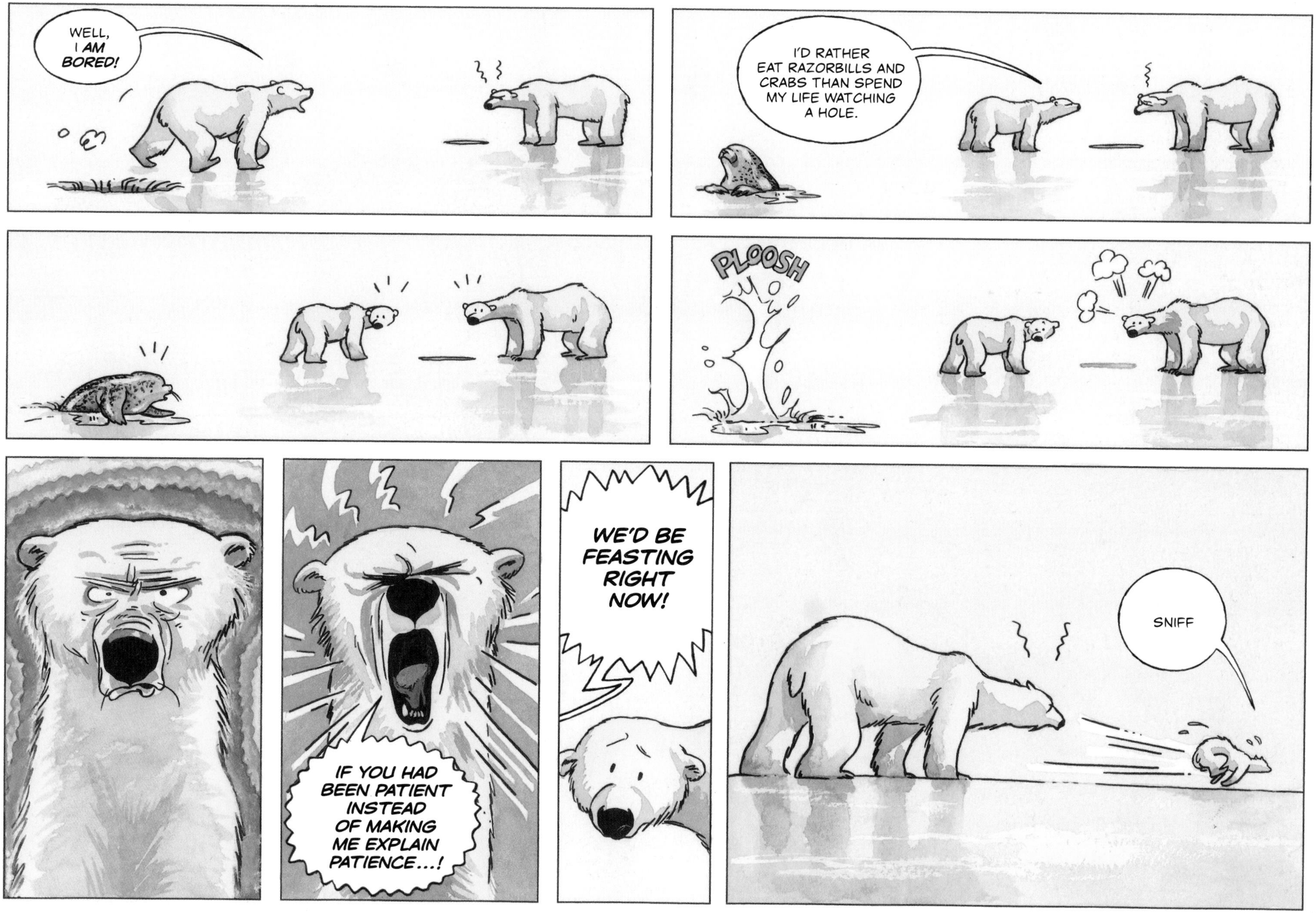
WELL, I AM BORED!
I'D RATHER EAT RAZORBILLS AND CRABS THAN SPEND MY LIFE WATCHING A HOLE.
PLOOSH
IF YOU HAD BEEN PATIENT INSTEAD OF MAKING ME EXPLAIN PATIENCE...!
WE'D BE FEASTING RIGHT NOW!
SNIFF

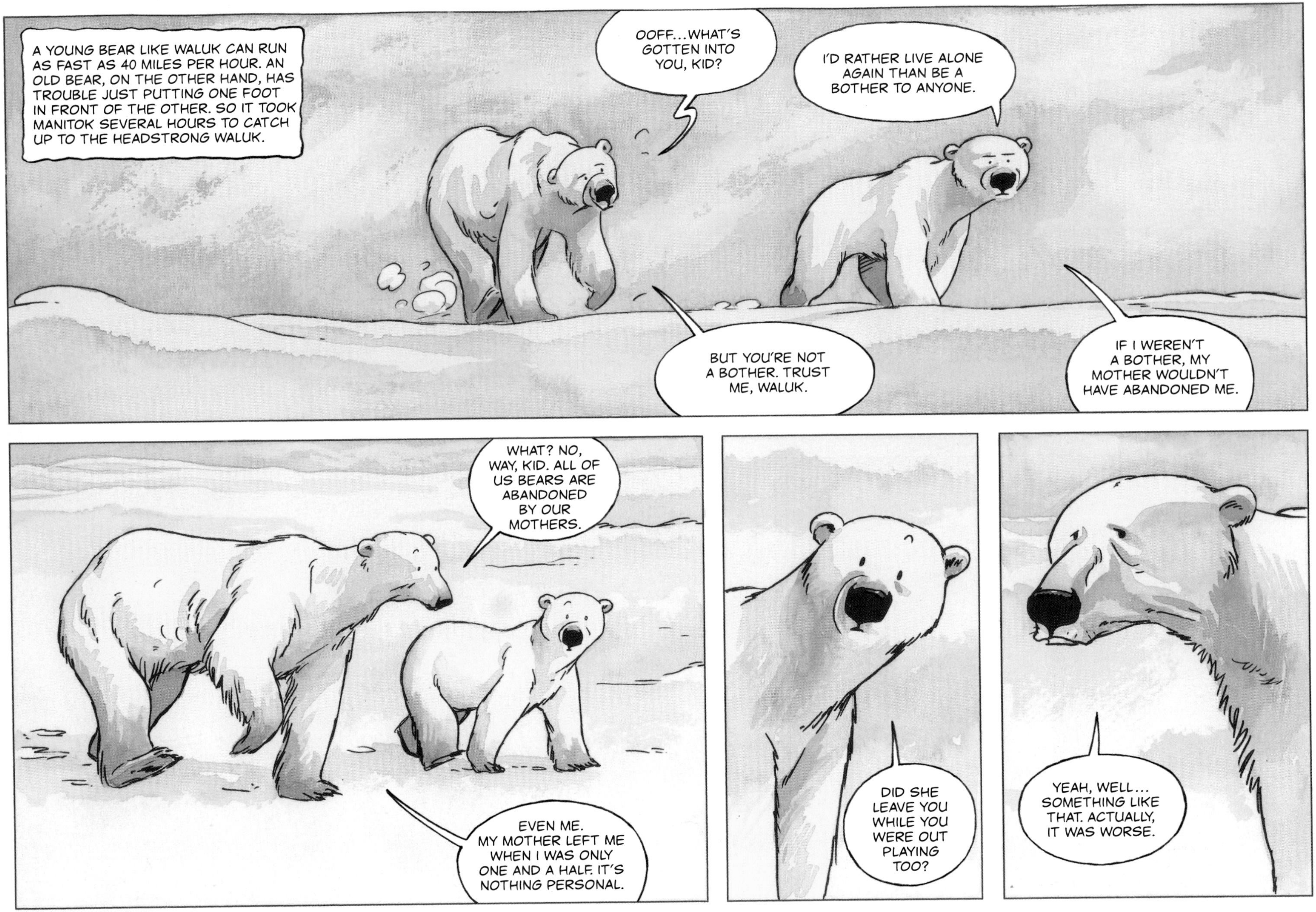
A YOUNG BEAR LIKE WALUK CAN RUN AS FAST AS 40 MILES PER HOUR. AN OLD BEAR, ON THE OTHER HAND, HAS TROUBLE JUST PUTTING ONE FOOT IN FRONT OF THE OTHER. SO IT TOOK MANITOK SEVERAL HOURS TO CATCH UP TO THE HEADSTRONG WALUK.
OOFF...WHAT'S GOTTEN INTO YOU, KID?
I'D RATHER LIVE ALONE AGAIN THAN BE A BOTHER TO ANYONE.
BUT YOU'RE NOT A BOTHER. TRUST ME, WALUK.
IF I WEREN'T A BOTHER, MY MOTHER WOULDN'T HAVE ABANDONED ME.
WHAT? NO, WAY, KID. ALL OF US BEARS ARE ABANDONED BY OUR MOTHERS.
EVEN ME. MY MOTHER LEFT ME WHEN I WAS ONLY ONE AND A HALF. IT'S NOTHING PERSONAL.
DID SHE LEAVE YOU WHILE YOU WERE OUT PLAYING TOO?
YEAH, WELL... SOMETHING LIKE THAT. ACTUALLY, IT WAS WORSE.

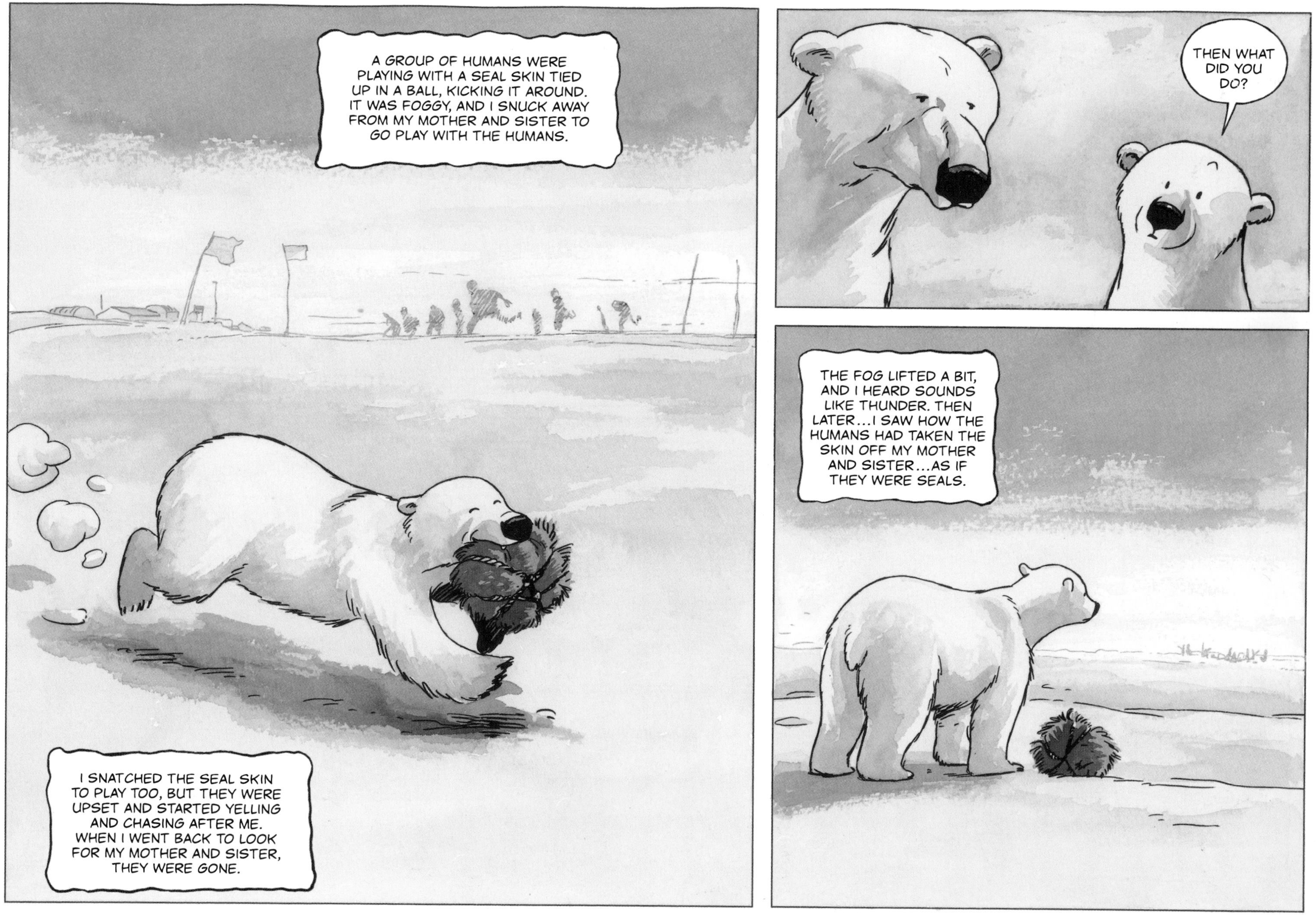
A GROUP OF HUMANS WERE PLAYING WITH A SEAL SKIN TIED UP IN A BALL, KICKING IT AROUND. IT WAS FOGGY, AND I SNUCK AWAY FROM MY MOTHER AND SISTER TO GO PLAY WITH THE HUMANS.
I SNATCHED THE SEAL SKIN TO PLAY TOO, BUT THEY WERE UPSET AND STARTED YELLING AND CHASING AFTER ME. WHEN I WENT BACK TO LOOK FOR MY MOTHER AND SISTER, THEY WERE GONE.
THEN WHAT DID YOU DO?
THE FOG LIFTED A BIT, AND I HEARD SOUNDS LIKE THUNDER. THEN LATER…I SAW HOW THE HUMANS HAD TAKEN THE SKIN OFF MY MOTHER AND SISTER…AS IF THEY WERE SEALS.

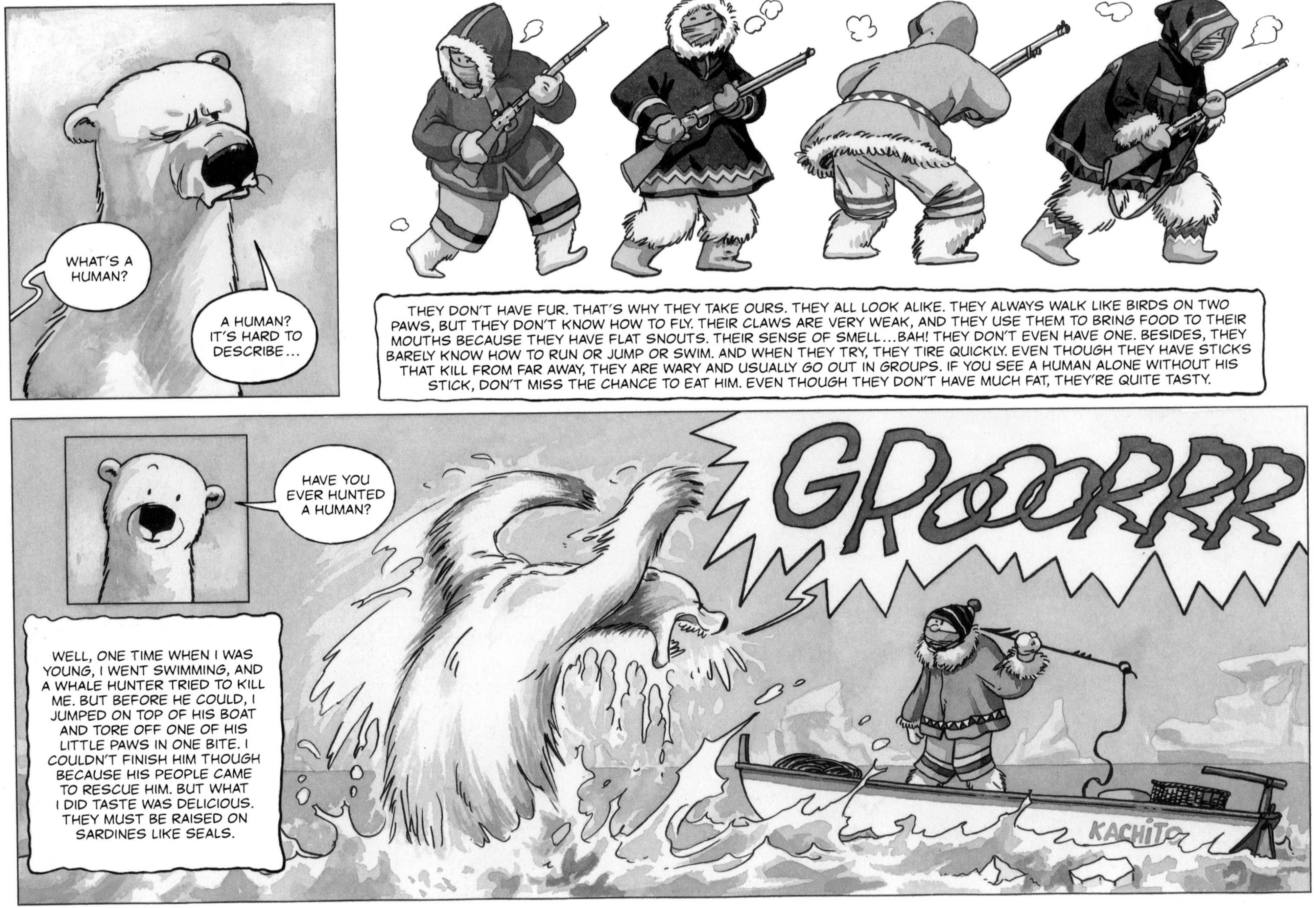
WHAT'S A HUMAN?
A HUMAN? IT'S HARD TO DESCRIBE...
THEY DON'T HAVE FUR. THAT'S WHY THEY TAKE OURS. THEY ALL LOOK ALIKE. THEY ALWAYS WALK LIKE BIRDS ON TWO PAWS, BUT THEY DON'T KNOW HOW TO FLY. THEIR CLAWS ARE VERY WEAK, AND THEY USE THEM TO BRING FOOD TO THEIR MOUTHS BECAUSE THEY HAVE FLAT SNOUTS. THEIR SENSE OF SMELL...BAH! THEY DON'T EVEN HAVE ONE. BESIDES, THEY BARELY KNOW HOW TO RUN OR JUMP OR SWIM. AND WHEN THEY TRY, THEY TIRE QUICKLY. EVEN THOUGH THEY HAVE STICKS THAT KILL FROM FAR AWAY, THEY ARE WARY AND USUALLY GO OUT IN GROUPS. IF YOU SEE A HUMAN ALONE WITHOUT HIS STICK, DON'T MISS THE CHANCE TO EAT HIM. EVEN THOUGH THEY DON'T HAVE MUCH FAT, THEY'RE QUITE TASTY.
HAVE YOU EVER HUNTED A HUMAN?
GROOORRR
WELL, ONE TIME WHEN I WAS YOUNG, I WENT SWIMMING, AND A WHALE HUNTER TRIED TO KILL ME. BUT BEFORE HE COULD, I JUMPED ON TOP OF HIS BOAT AND TORE OFF ONE OF HIS LITTLE PAWS IN ONE BITE. I COULDN'T FINISH HIM THOUGH BECAUSE HIS PEOPLE CAME TO RESCUE HIM. BUT WHAT I DID TASTE WAS DELICIOUS. THEY MUST BE RAISED ON SARDINES LIKE SEALS.
KACHITO

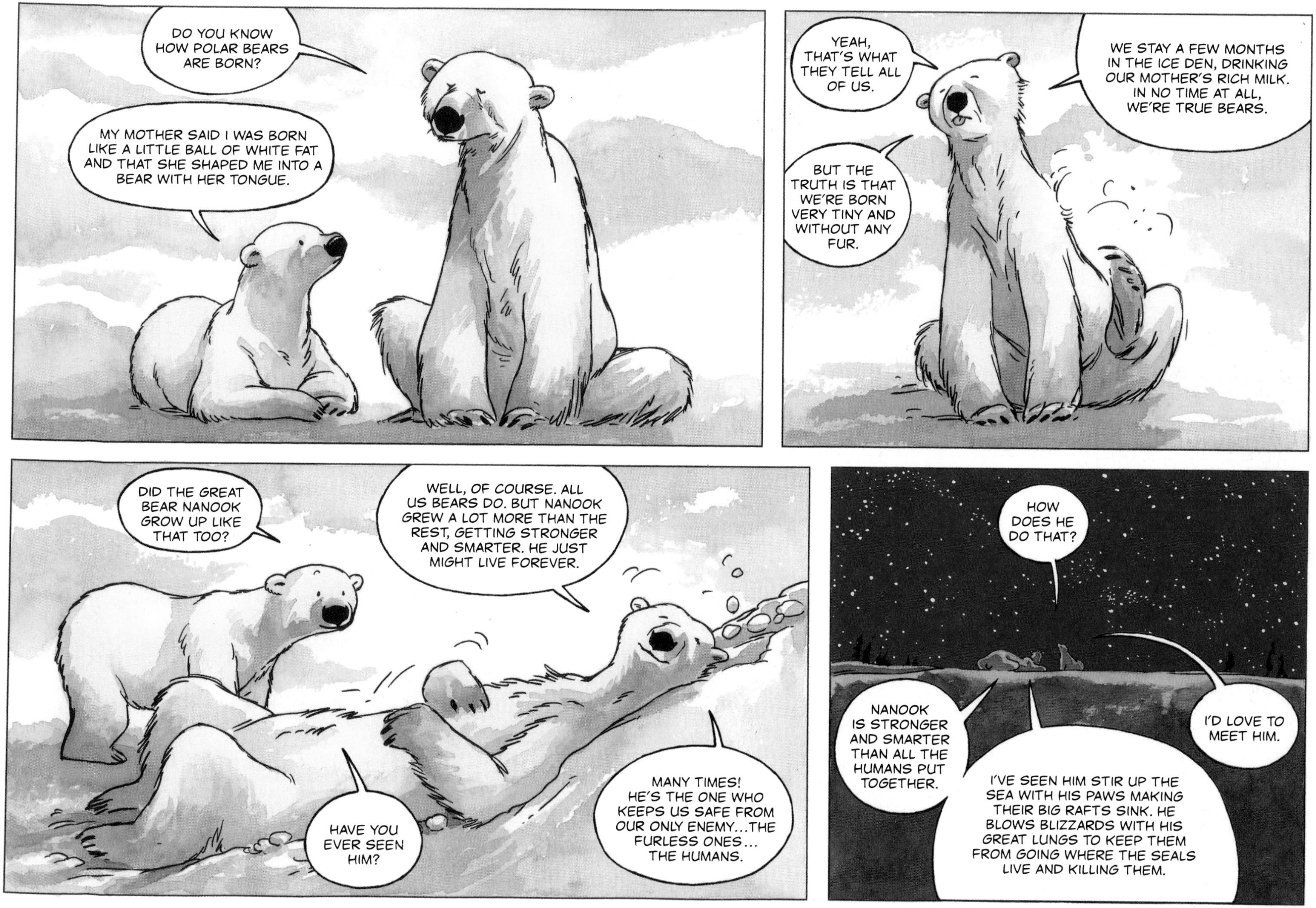
DO YOU KNOW HOW POLAR BEARS ARE BORN?
MY MOTHER SAID I WAS BORN LIKE A LITTLE BALL OF WHITE FAT AND THAT SHE SHAPED ME INTO A BEAR WITH HER TONGUE.
YEAH, THAT'S WHAT THEY TELL ALL OF US.
BUT THE TRUTH IS THAT WE'RE BORN VERY TINY AND WITHOUT ANY FUR.
WE STAY A FEW MONTHS IN THE ICE DEN, DRINKING OUR MOTHER'S RICH MILK. IN NO TIME AT ALL, WE'RE TRUE BEARS.
DID THE GREAT BEAR NANOOK GROW UP LIKE THAT TOO?
WELL, OF COURSE. ALL US BEARS DO. BUT NANOOK GREW A LOT MORE THAN THE REST, GETTING STRONGER AND SMARTER. HE JUST MIGHT LIVE FOREVER.
HAVE YOU EVER SEEN HIM?
MANY TIMES! HE'S THE ONE WHO KEEPS US SAFE FROM OUR ONLY ENEMY...THE FURLESS ONES... THE HUMANS.
HOW DOES HE DO THAT?
NANOOK IS STRONGER AND SMARTER THAN ALL THE HUMANS PUT TOGETHER.
I'VE SEEN HIM STIR UP THE SEA WITH HIS PAWS MAKING THEIR BIG RAFTS SINK. HE BLOWS BLIZZARDS WITH HIS GREAT LUNGS TO KEEP THEM FROM GOING WHERE THE SEALS LIVE AND KILLING THEM.
I'D LOVE TO MEET HIM.

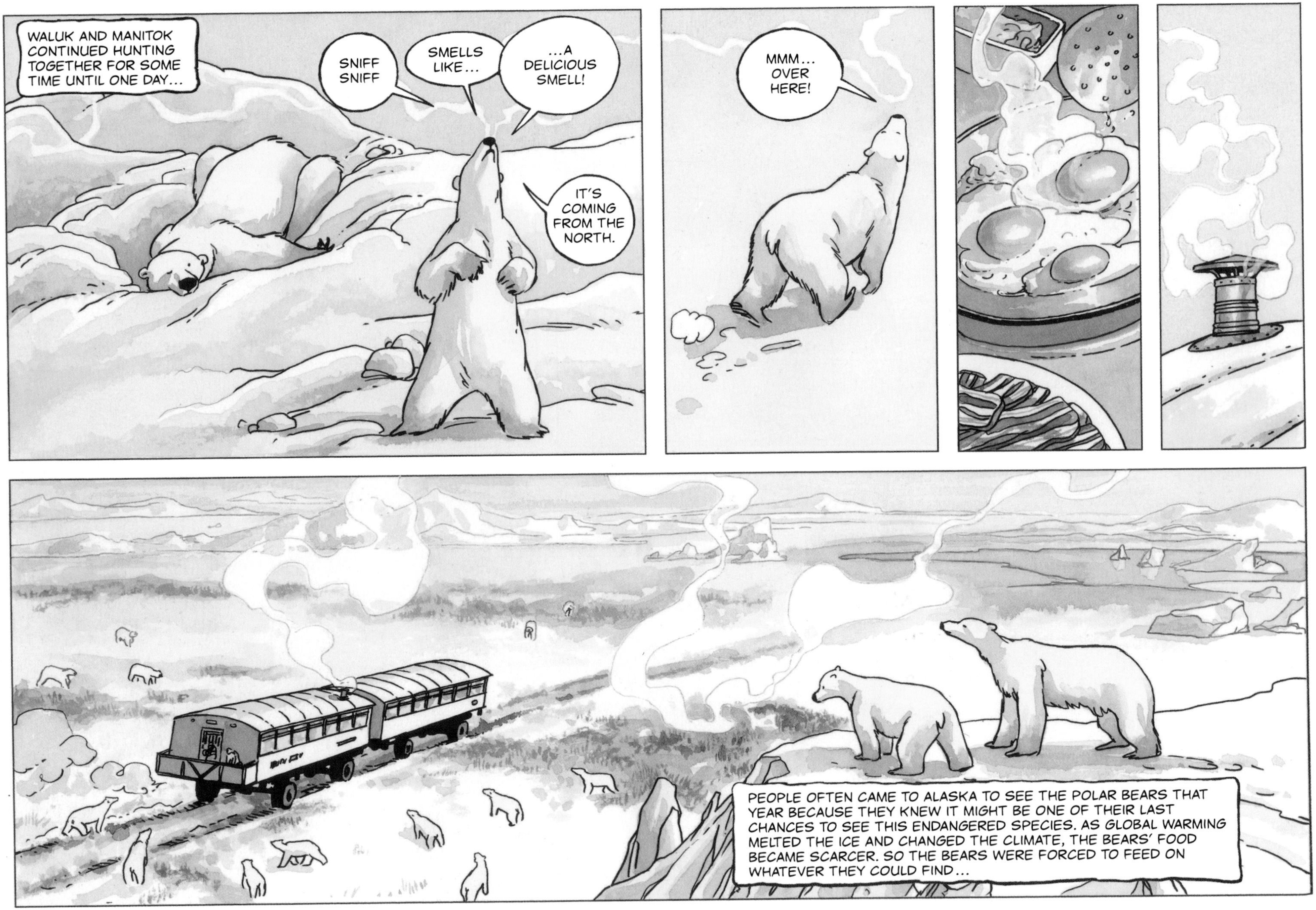
WALUK AND MANITOK CONTINUED HUNTING TOGETHER FOR SOME TIME UNTIL ONE DAY...
SNIFF SNIFF
SMELLS LIKE...
...A DELICIOUS SMELL!
IT'S COMING FROM THE NORTH.
MMM... OVER HERE!
PEOPLE OFTEN CAME TO ALASKA TO SEE THE POLAR BEARS THAT YEAR BECAUSE THEY KNEW IT MIGHT BE ONE OF THEIR LAST CHANCES TO SEE THIS ENDANGERED SPECIES. AS GLOBAL WARMING MELTED THE ICE AND CHANGED THE CLIMATE, THE BEARS' FOOD BECAME SCARCER. SO THE BEARS WERE FORCED TO FEED ON WHATEVER THEY COULD FIND...

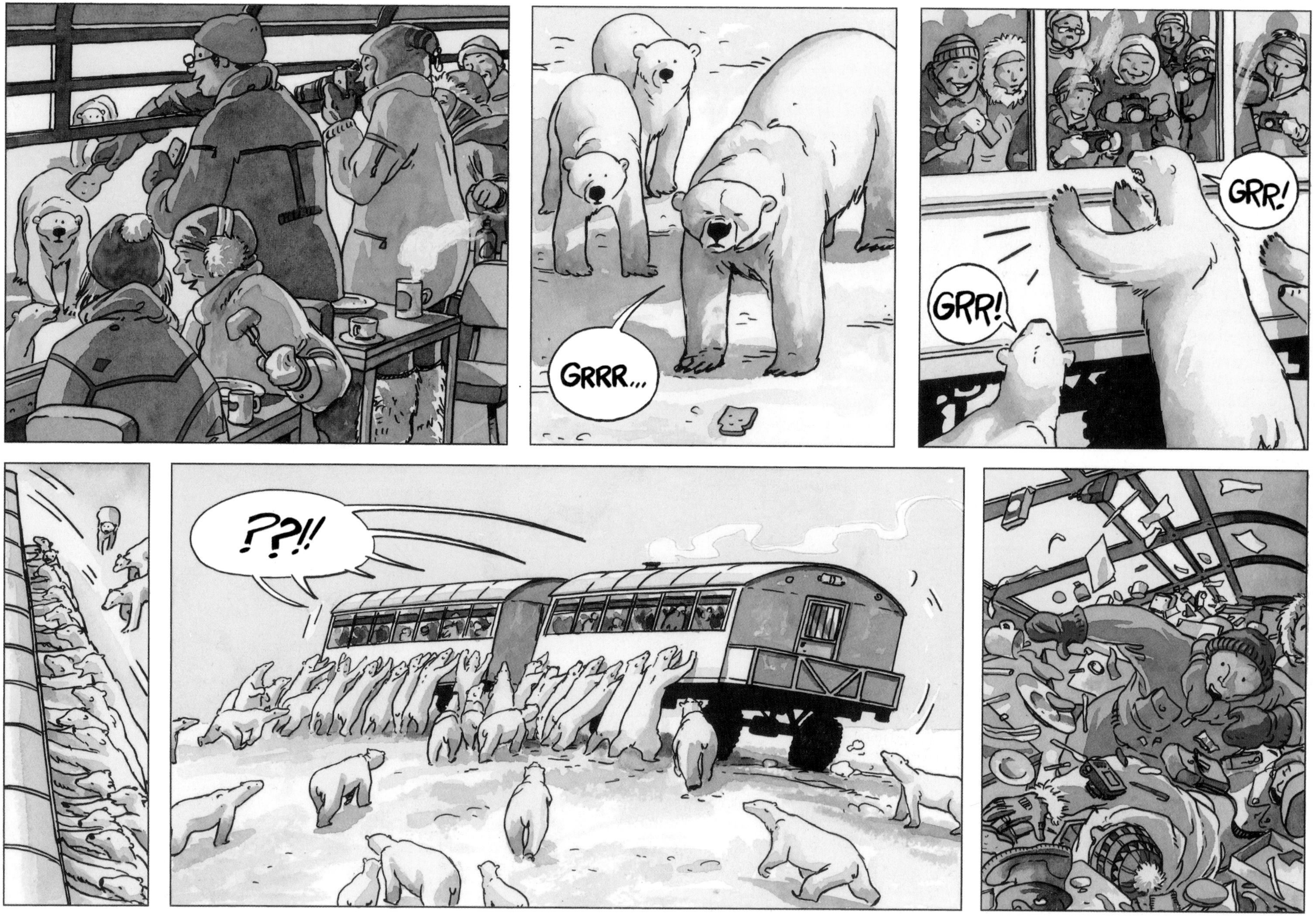
GRRR...
GRR!
GRR!
??!!

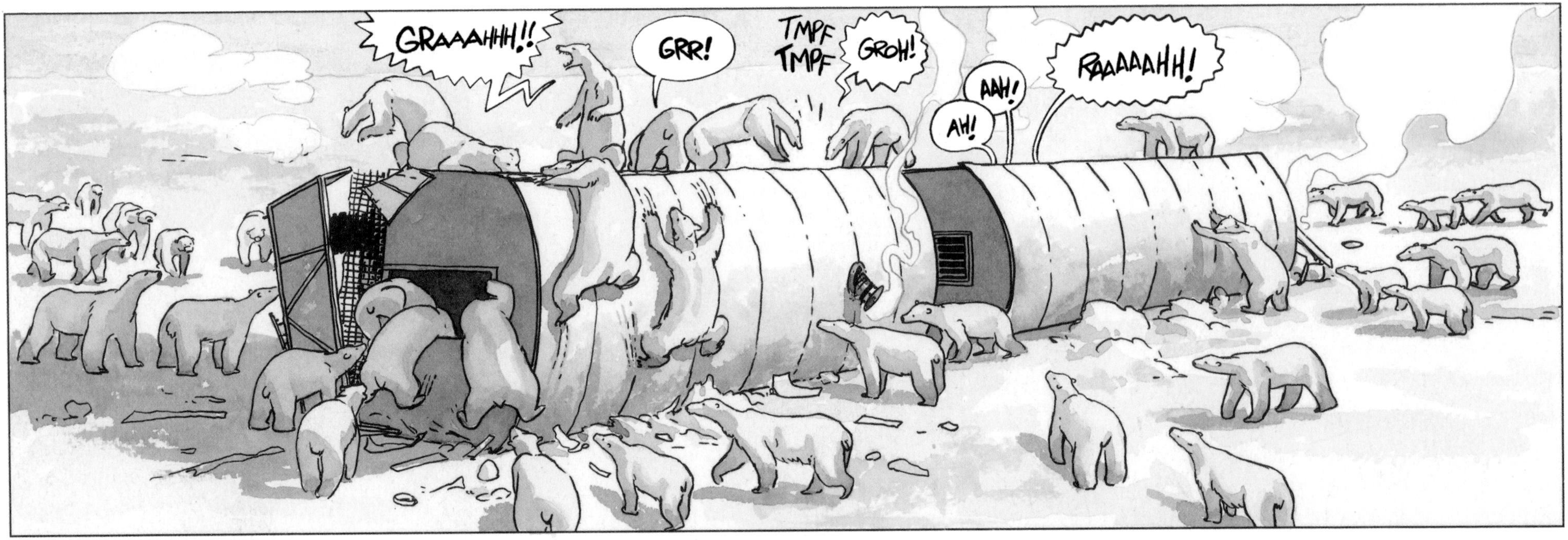
GRAAAHHH!!
GRR!
TMPF TMPF
GROH!
AH!
AAH!
RAAAAAHH!

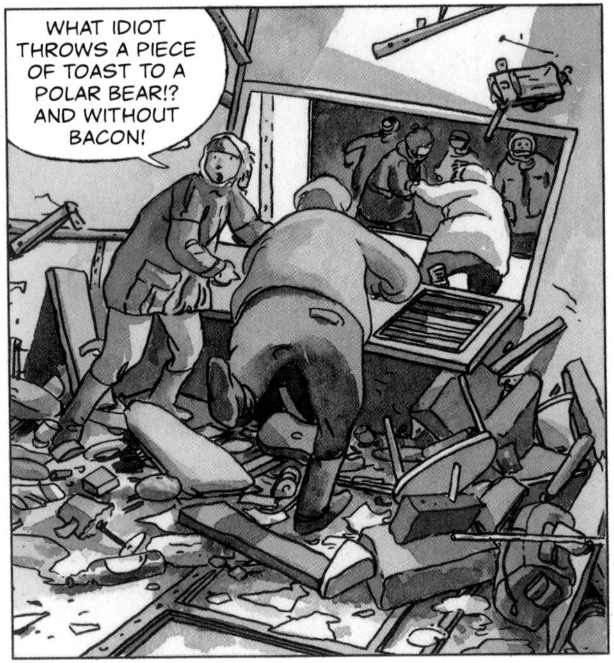
WHAT IDIOT THROWS A PIECE OF TOAST TO A POLAR BEAR!? AND WITHOUT BACON!

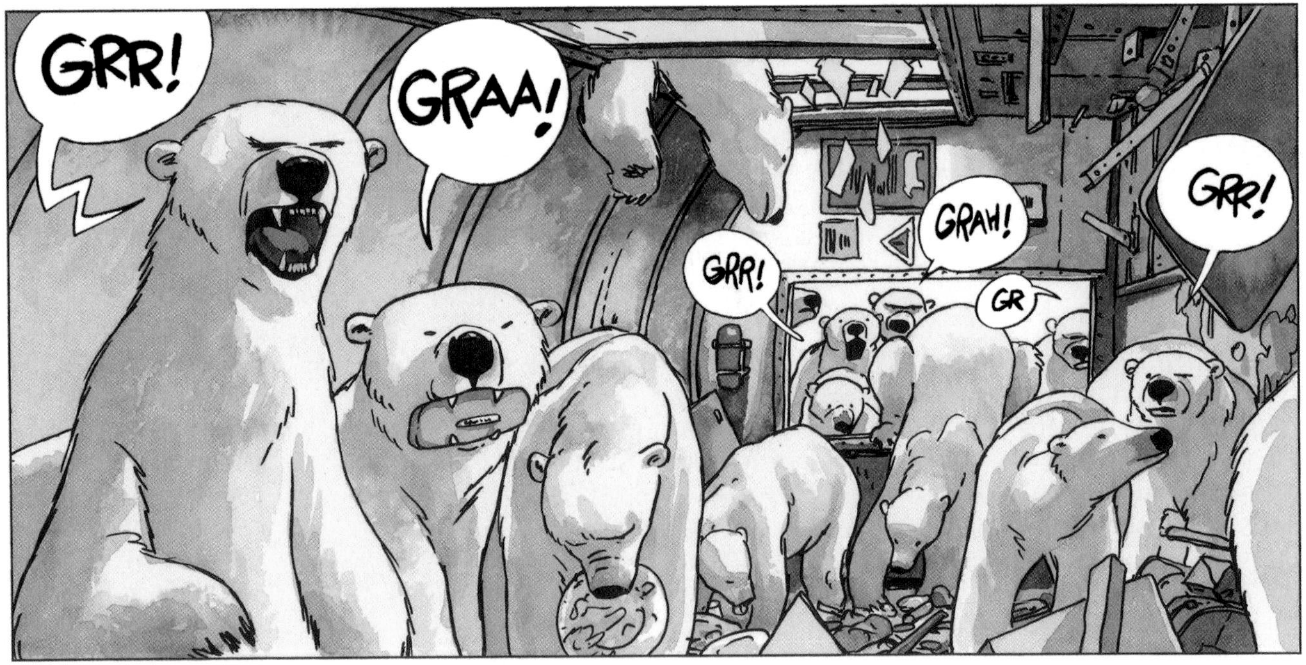
GRR!
GRAA!
GRR!
GRAH!
GR
GRR!

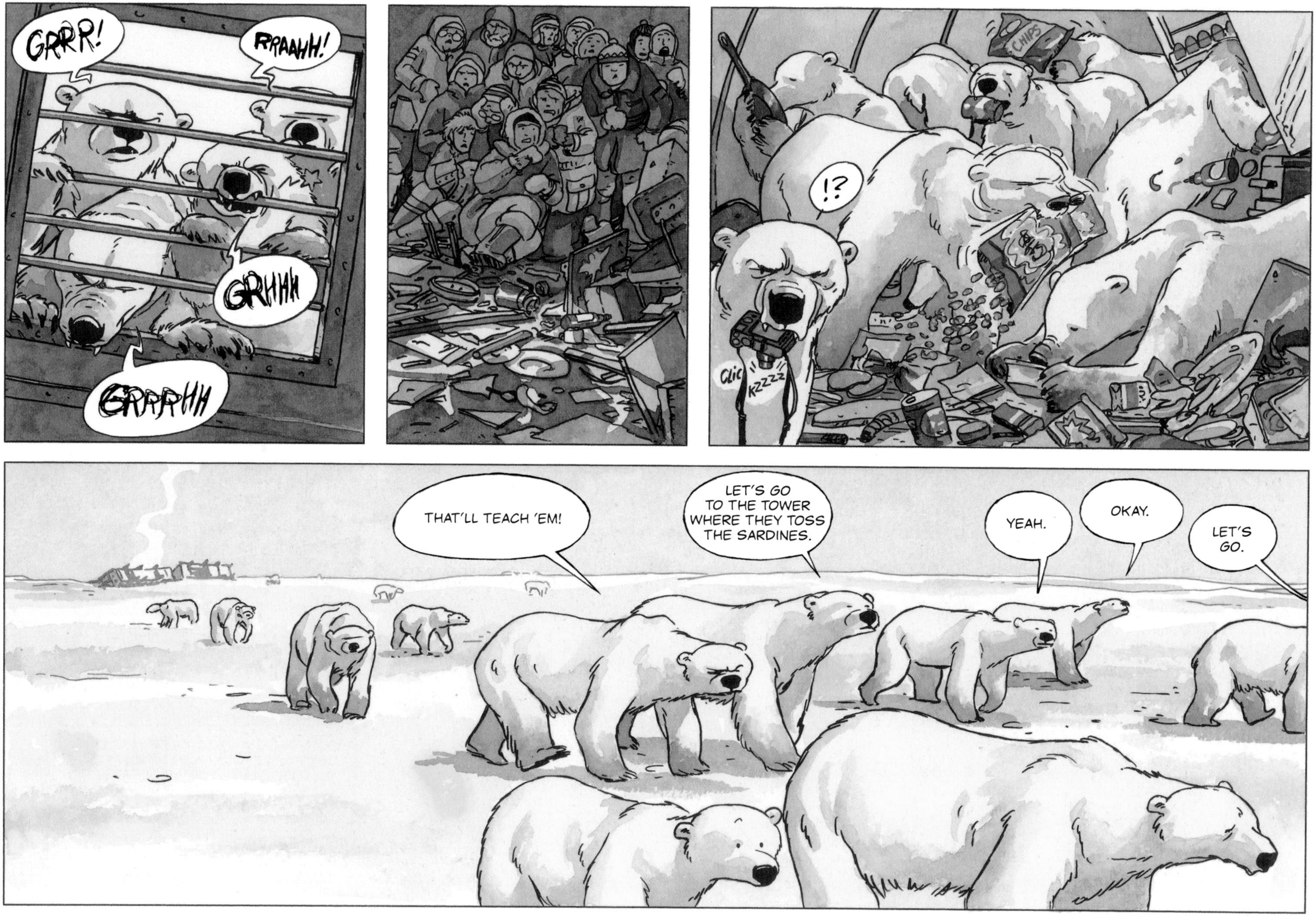
GRRR!
RRAAHH!
GRHHH
GRRRRHH
!?
CHIPS
CLIC
KZZZZ
THAT'LL TEACH 'EM!
LET'S GO TO THE TOWER WHERE THEY TOSS THE SARDINES.
YEAH.
OKAY.
LET'S GO.

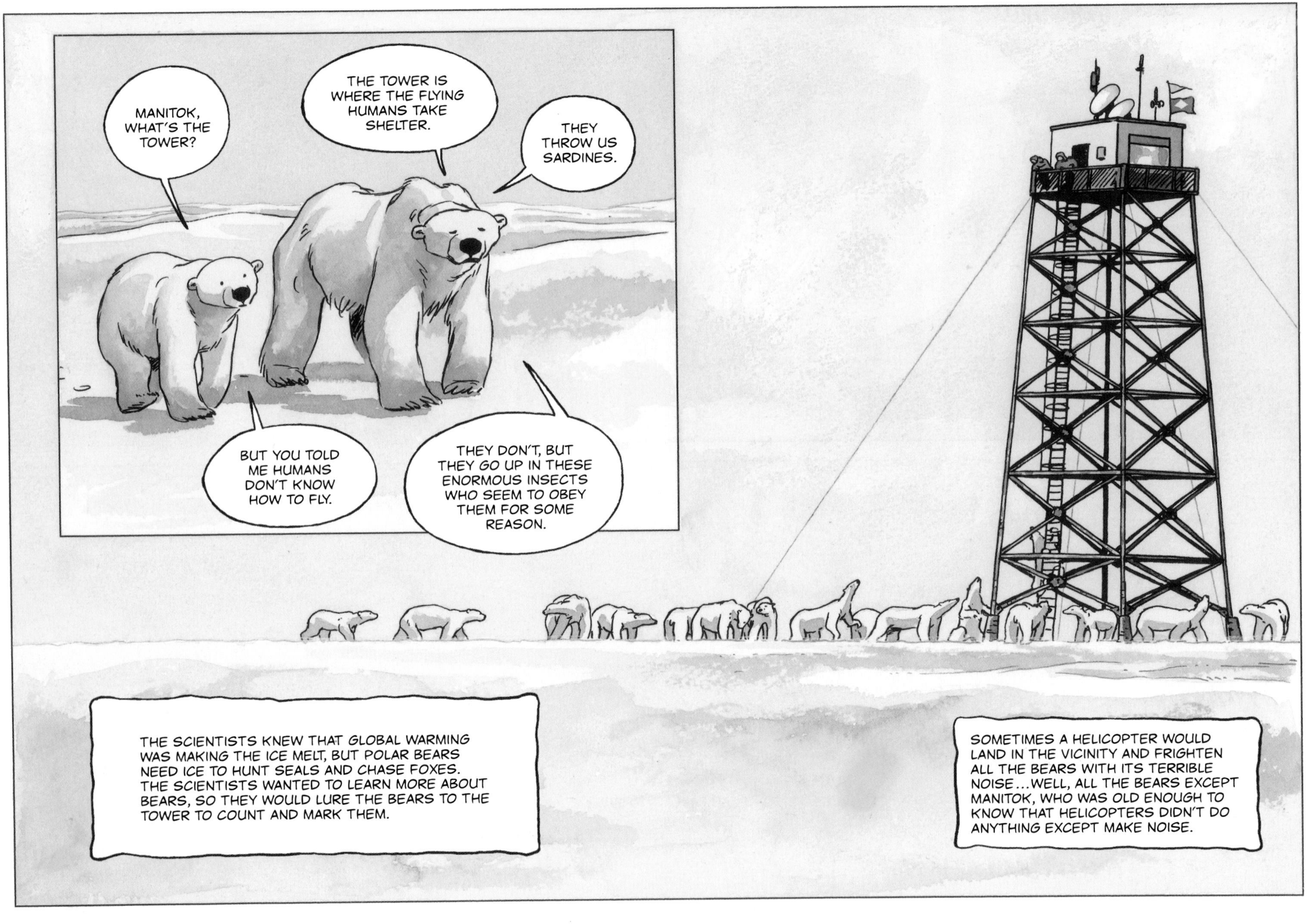
MANITOK, WHAT'S THE TOWER?
THE TOWER IS WHERE THE FLYING HUMANS TAKE SHELTER.
THEY THROW US SARDINES.
BUT YOU TOLD ME HUMANS DON'T KNOW HOW TO FLY.
THEY DON'T, BUT THEY GO UP IN THESE ENORMOUS INSECTS WHO SEEM TO OBEY THEM FOR SOME REASON.
THE SCIENTISTS KNEW THAT GLOBAL WARMING WAS MAKING THE ICE MELT, BUT POLAR BEARS NEED ICE TO HUNT SEALS AND CHASE FOXES. THE SCIENTISTS WANTED TO LEARN MORE ABOUT BEARS, SO THEY WOULD LURE THE BEARS TO THE TOWER TO COUNT AND MARK THEM.
SOMETIMES A HELICOPTER WOULD LAND IN THE VICINITY AND FRIGHTEN ALL THE BEARS WITH ITS TERRIBLE NOISE...WELL, ALL THE BEARS EXCEPT MANITOK, WHO WAS OLD ENOUGH TO KNOW THAT HELICOPTERS DIDN'T DO ANYTHING EXCEPT MAKE NOISE.

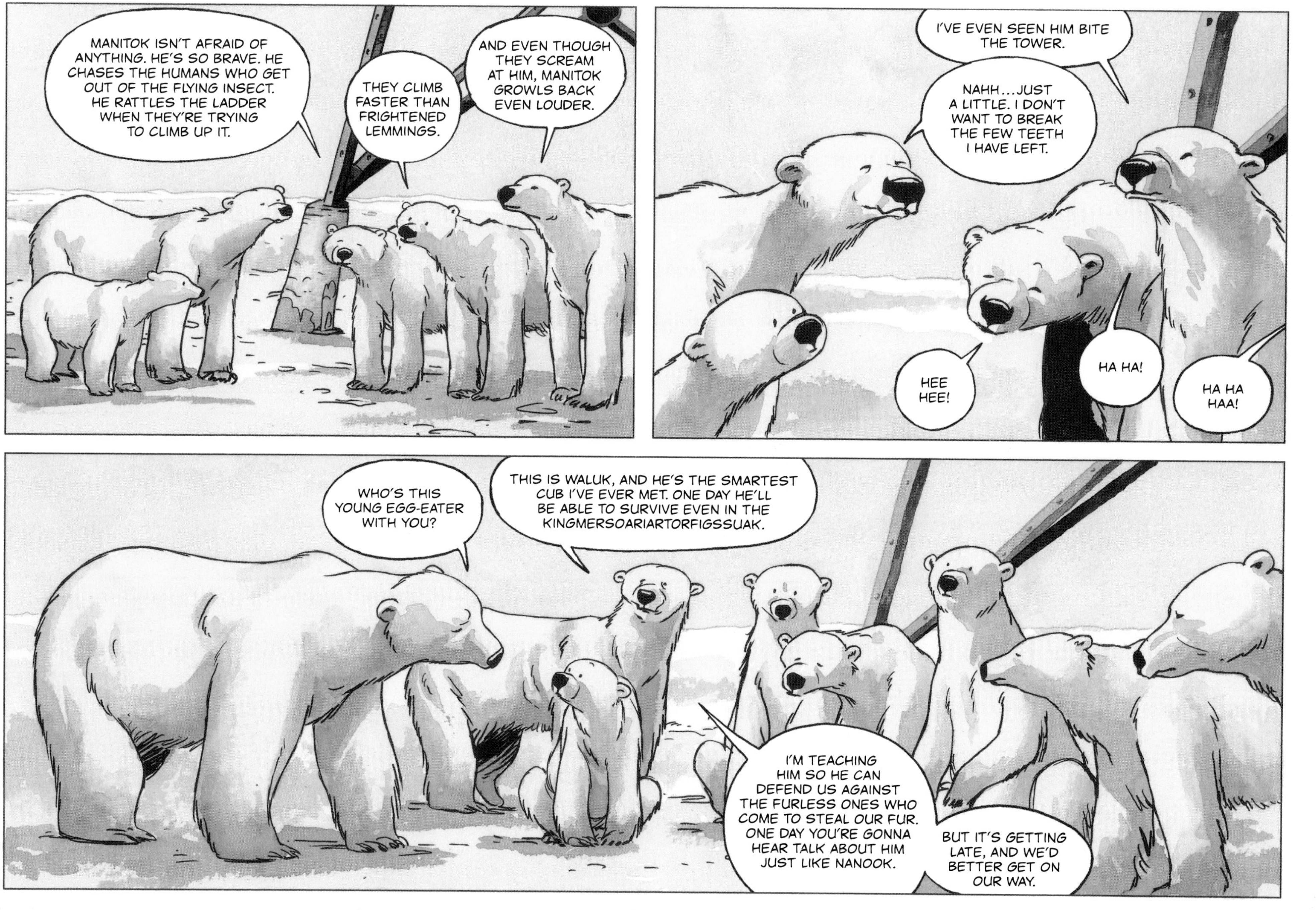

MANITOK ISN'T AFRAID OF ANYTHING. HE'S SO BRAVE. HE CHASES THE HUMANS WHO GET OUT OF THE FLYING INSECT. HE RATTLES THE LADDER WHEN THEY'RE TRYING TO CLIMB UP IT.
THEY CLIMB FASTER THAN FRIGHTENED LEMMINGS.
AND EVEN THOUGH THEY SCREAM AT HIM, MANITOK GROWLS BACK EVEN LOUDER.
I'VE EVEN SEEN HIM BITE THE TOWER.
NAHH...JUST A LITTLE. I DON'T WANT TO BREAK THE FEW TEETH I HAVE LEFT.
HEE HEE!
HA HA!
HA HA HAA!
WHO'S THIS YOUNG EGG-EATER WITH YOU?
THIS IS WALUK, AND HE'S THE SMARTEST CUB I'VE EVER MET. ONE DAY HE'LL BE ABLE TO SURVIVE EVEN IN THE KINGMERSOARIARTORFIGSSUAK.
I'M TEACHING HIM SO HE CAN DEFEND US AGAINST THE FURLESS ONES WHO COME TO STEAL OUR FUR. ONE DAY YOU'RE GONNA HEAR TALK ABOUT HIM JUST LIKE NANOOK.
BUT IT'S GETTING LATE, AND WE'D BETTER GET ON OUR WAY.

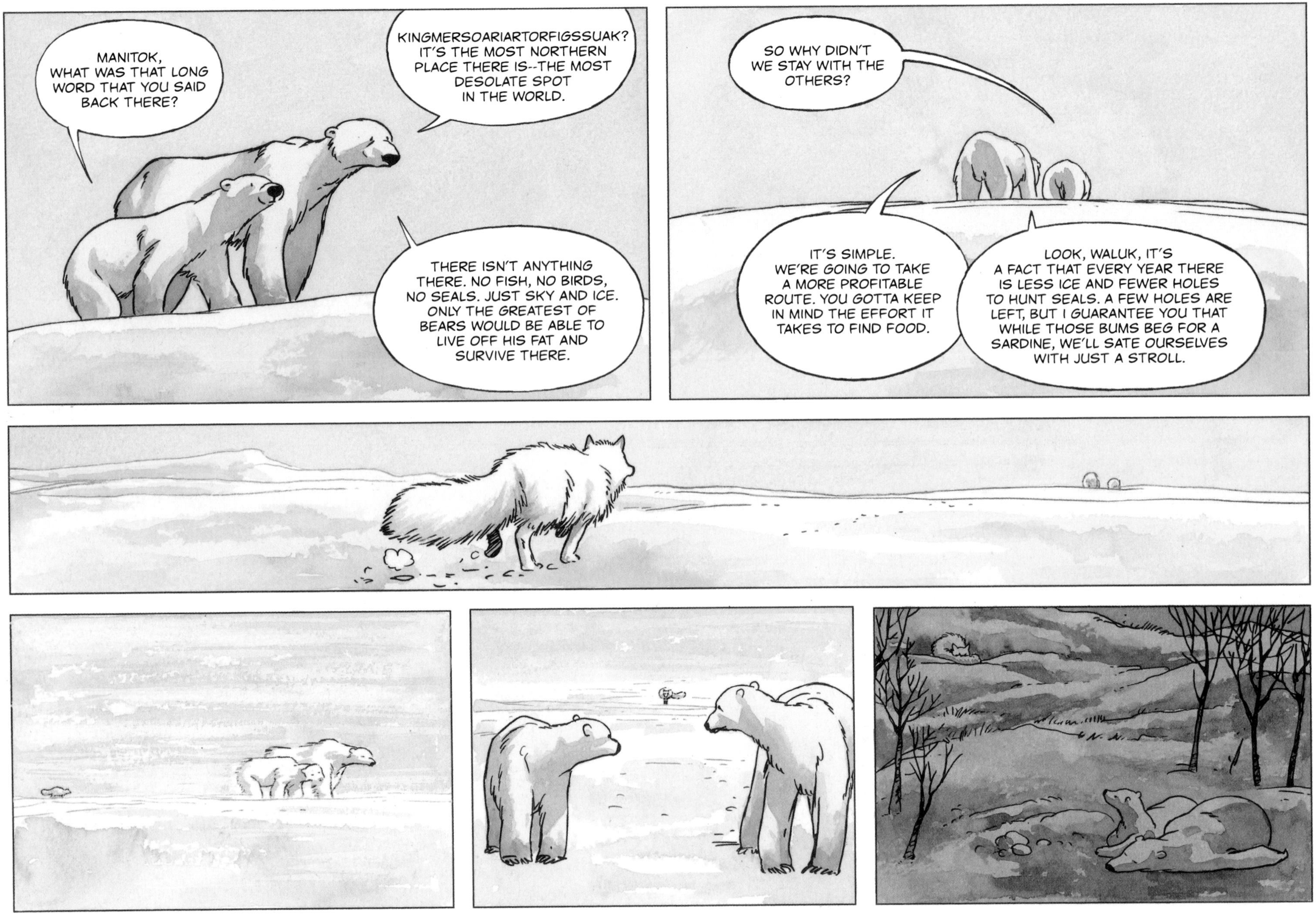

MANITOK, WHAT WAS THAT LONG WORD THAT YOU SAID BACK THERE?
KINGMERSOARIARTORFIGSSUAK? IT'S THE MOST NORTHERN PLACE THERE IS--THE MOST DESOLATE SPOT IN THE WORLD.
THERE ISN'T ANYTHING THERE. NO FISH, NO BIRDS, NO SEALS. JUST SKY AND ICE. ONLY THE GREATEST OF BEARS WOULD BE ABLE TO LIVE OFF HIS FAT AND SURVIVE THERE.
SO WHY DIDN'T WE STAY WITH THE OTHERS?
IT'S SIMPLE. WE'RE GOING TO TAKE A MORE PROFITABLE ROUTE. YOU GOTTA KEEP IN MIND THE EFFORT IT TAKES TO FIND FOOD.
LOOK, WALUK, IT'S A FACT THAT EVERY YEAR THERE IS LESS ICE AND FEWER HOLES TO HUNT SEALS. A FEW HOLES ARE LEFT, BUT I GUARANTEE YOU THAT WHILE THOSE BUMS BEG FOR A SARDINE, WE'LL SATE OURSELVES WITH JUST A STROLL.

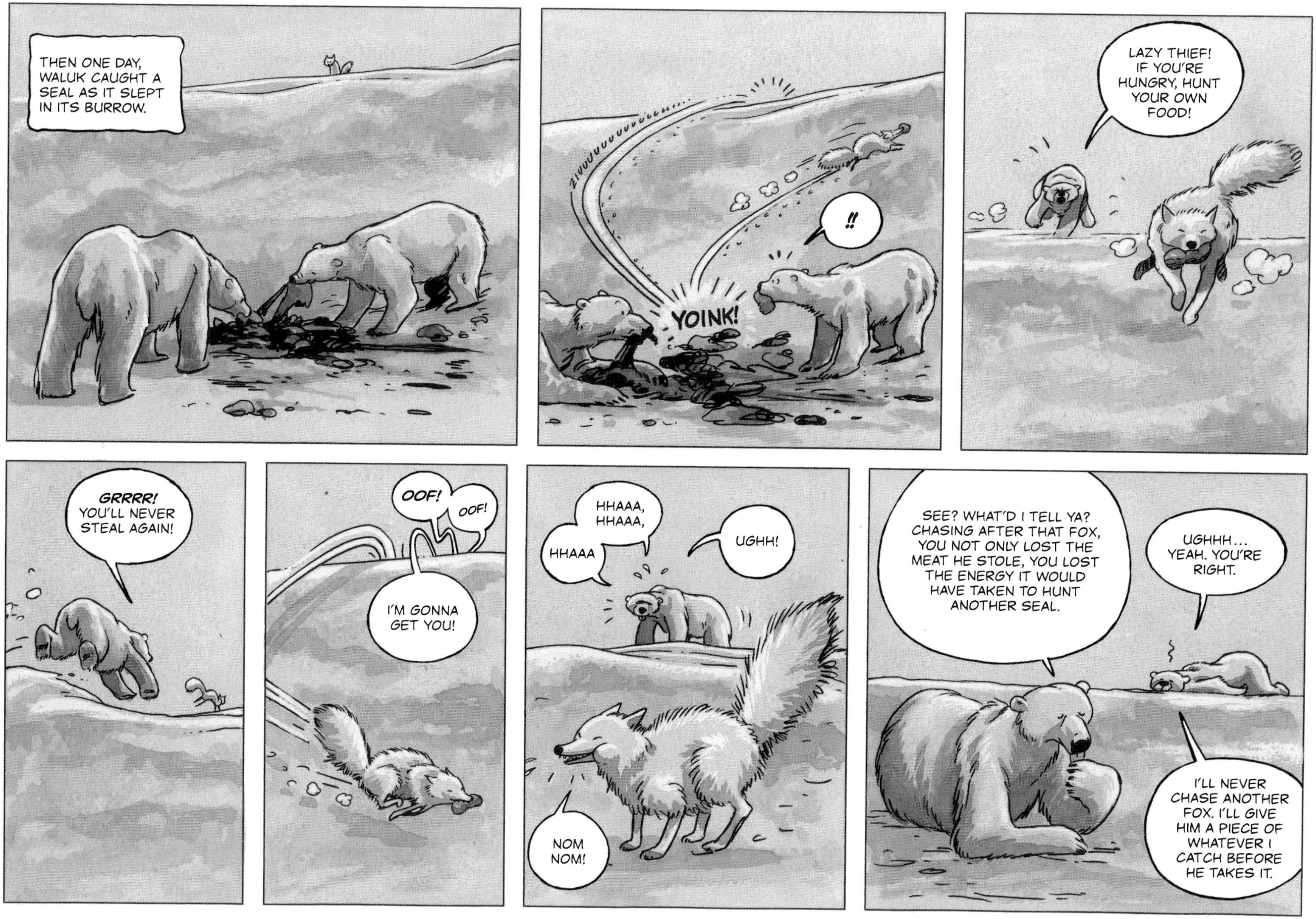
THEN ONE DAY, WALUK CAUGHT A SEAL AS IT SLEPT IN ITS BURROW.
YOINK!
!!
LAZY THIEF! IF YOU'RE HUNGRY, HUNT YOUR OWN FOOD!
GRRRR! YOU'LL NEVER STEAL AGAIN!
OOF!
OOF!
I'M GONNA GET YOU!
HHAAA, HHAAA,
HHAAA
UGHH!
NOM NOM!
SEE? WHAT'D I TELL YA? CHASING AFTER THAT FOX, YOU NOT ONLY LOST THE MEAT HE STOLE, YOU LOST THE ENERGY IT WOULD HAVE TAKEN TO HUNT ANOTHER SEAL.
UGHHH... YEAH. YOU'RE RIGHT.
I'LL NEVER CHASE ANOTHER FOX. I'LL GIVE HIM A PIECE OF WHATEVER I CATCH BEFORE HE TAKES IT.

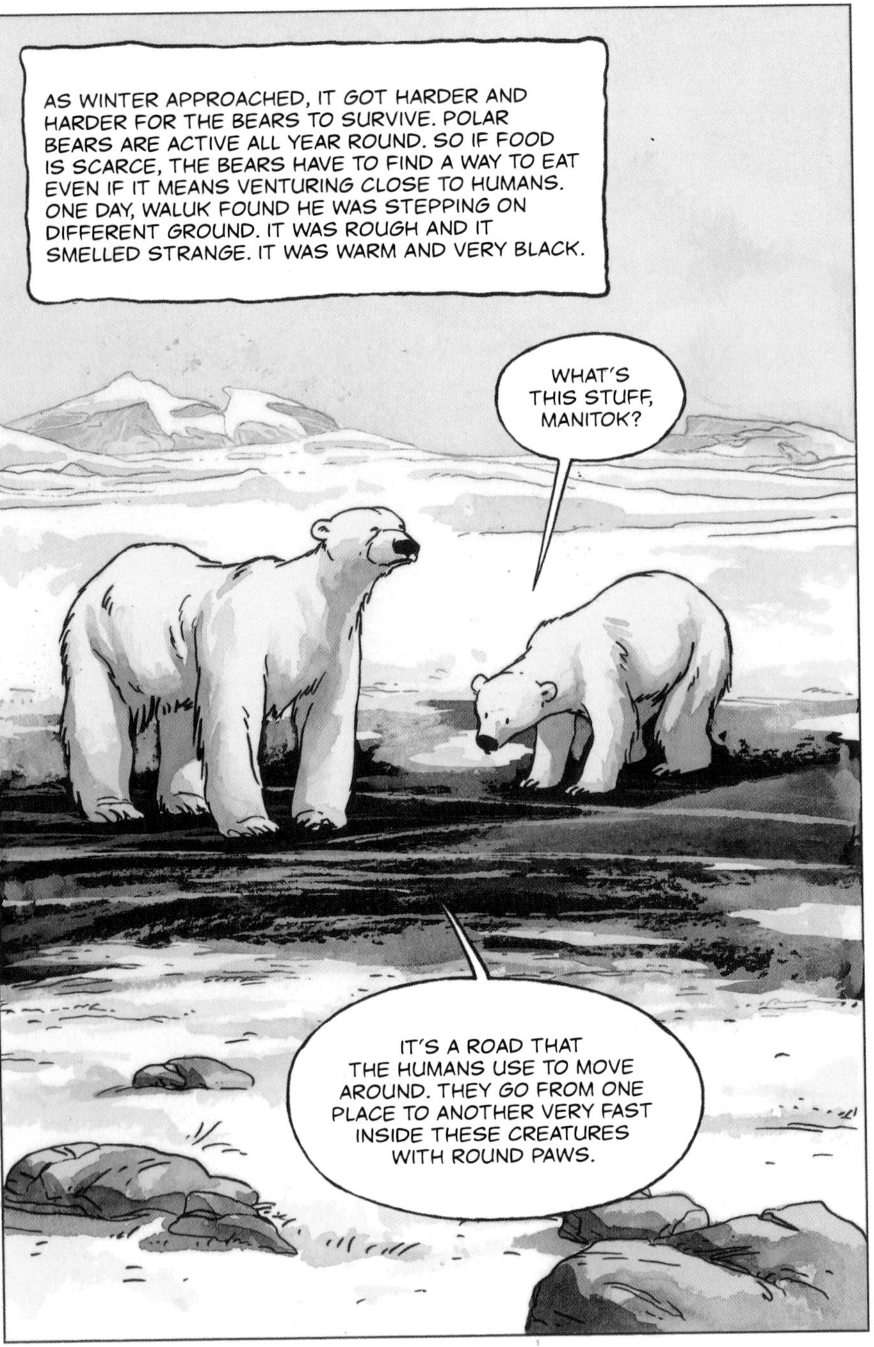
AS WINTER APPROACHED, IT GOT HARDER AND HARDER FOR THE BEARS TO SURVIVE. POLAR BEARS ARE ACTIVE ALL YEAR ROUND. SO IF FOOD IS SCARCE, THE BEARS HAVE TO FIND A WAY TO EAT EVEN IF IT MEANS VENTURING CLOSE TO HUMANS. ONE DAY, WALUK FOUND HE WAS STEPPING ON DIFFERENT GROUND. IT WAS ROUGH AND IT SMELLED STRANGE. IT WAS WARM AND VERY BLACK.
WHAT'S THIS STUFF, MANITOK?
IT'S A ROAD THAT THE HUMANS USE TO MOVE AROUND. THEY GO FROM ONE PLACE TO ANOTHER VERY FAST INSIDE THESE CREATURES WITH ROUND PAWS.

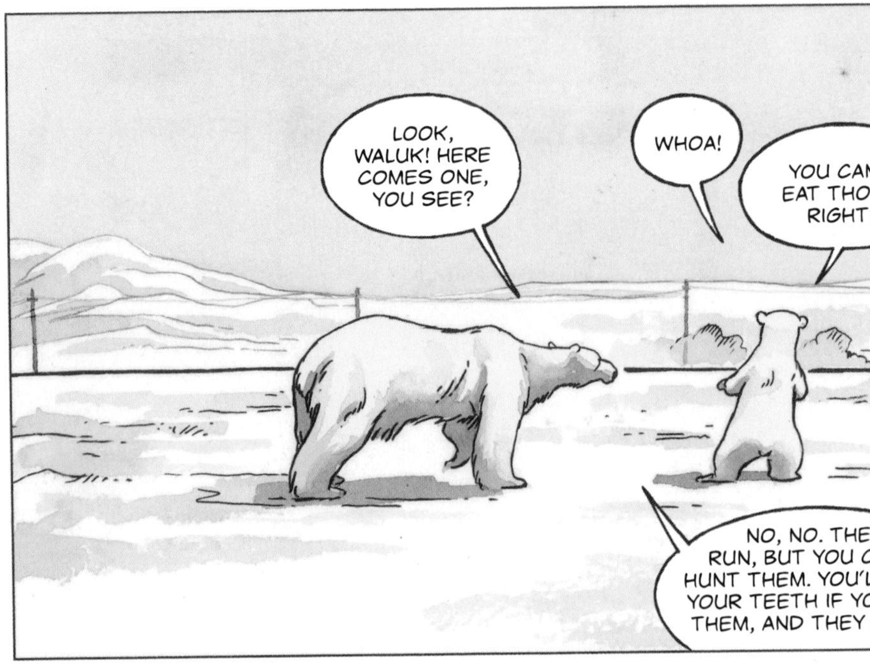
LOOK, WALUK! HERE COMES ONE, YOU SEE?
WHOA!
YOU CAN'T EAT THOSE, RIGHT?
NO, NO. THEY RUN, BUT YOU CAN'T HUNT THEM. YOU'LL LOSE YOUR TEETH IF YOU BITE THEM, AND THEY STINK.

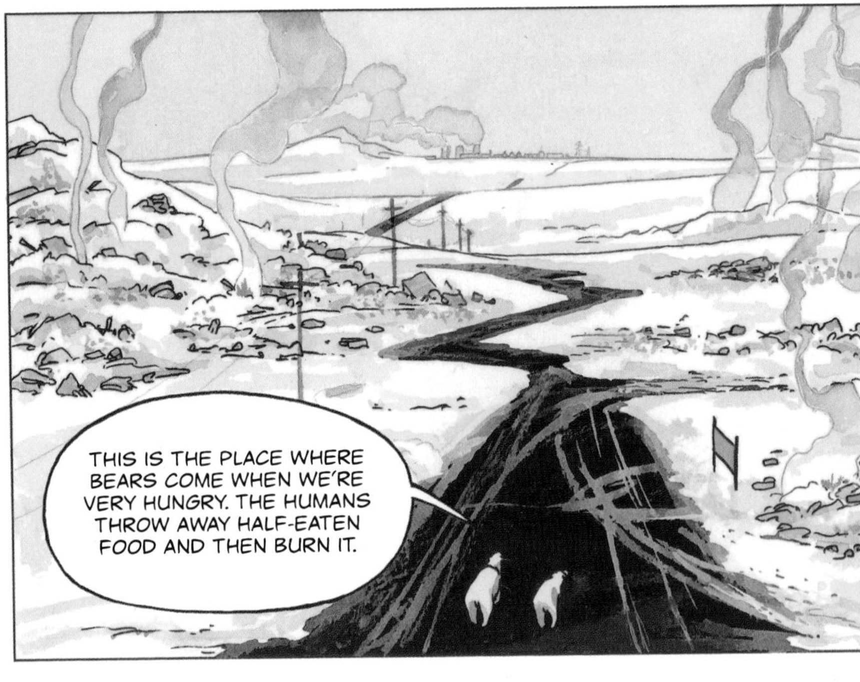
THIS IS THE PLACE WHERE BEARS COME WHEN WE'RE VERY HUNGRY. THE HUMANS THROW AWAY HALF-EATEN FOOD AND THEN BURN IT.

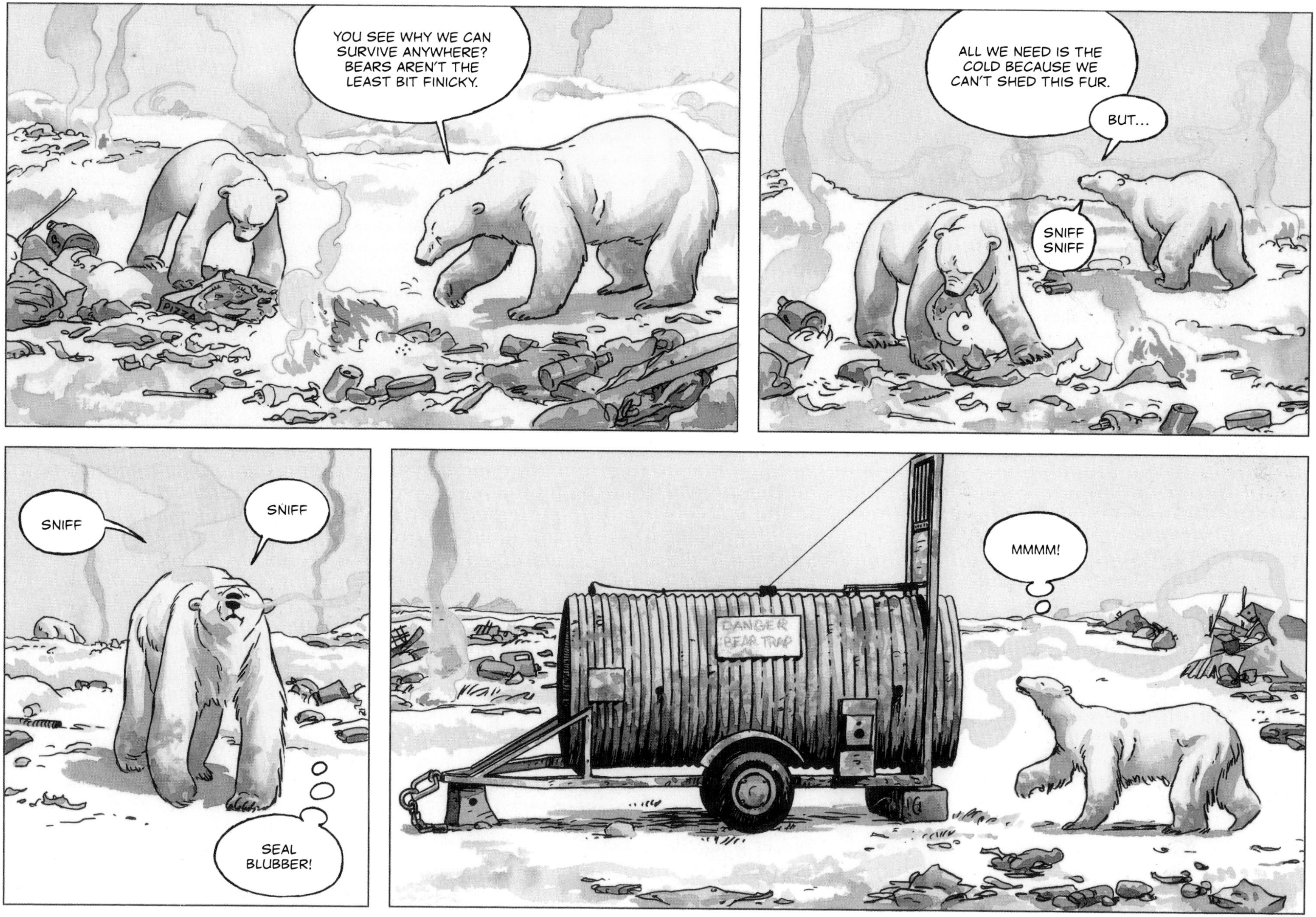
YOU SEE WHY WE CAN SURVIVE ANYWHERE? BEARS AREN'T THE LEAST BIT FINICKY.
PIZZA
ALL WE NEED IS THE COLD BECAUSE WE CAN'T SHED THIS FUR.
BUT…
SNIFF SNIFF
SNIFF
SNIFF
SEAL BLUBBER!
MMMM!
DANGER BEAR TRAP

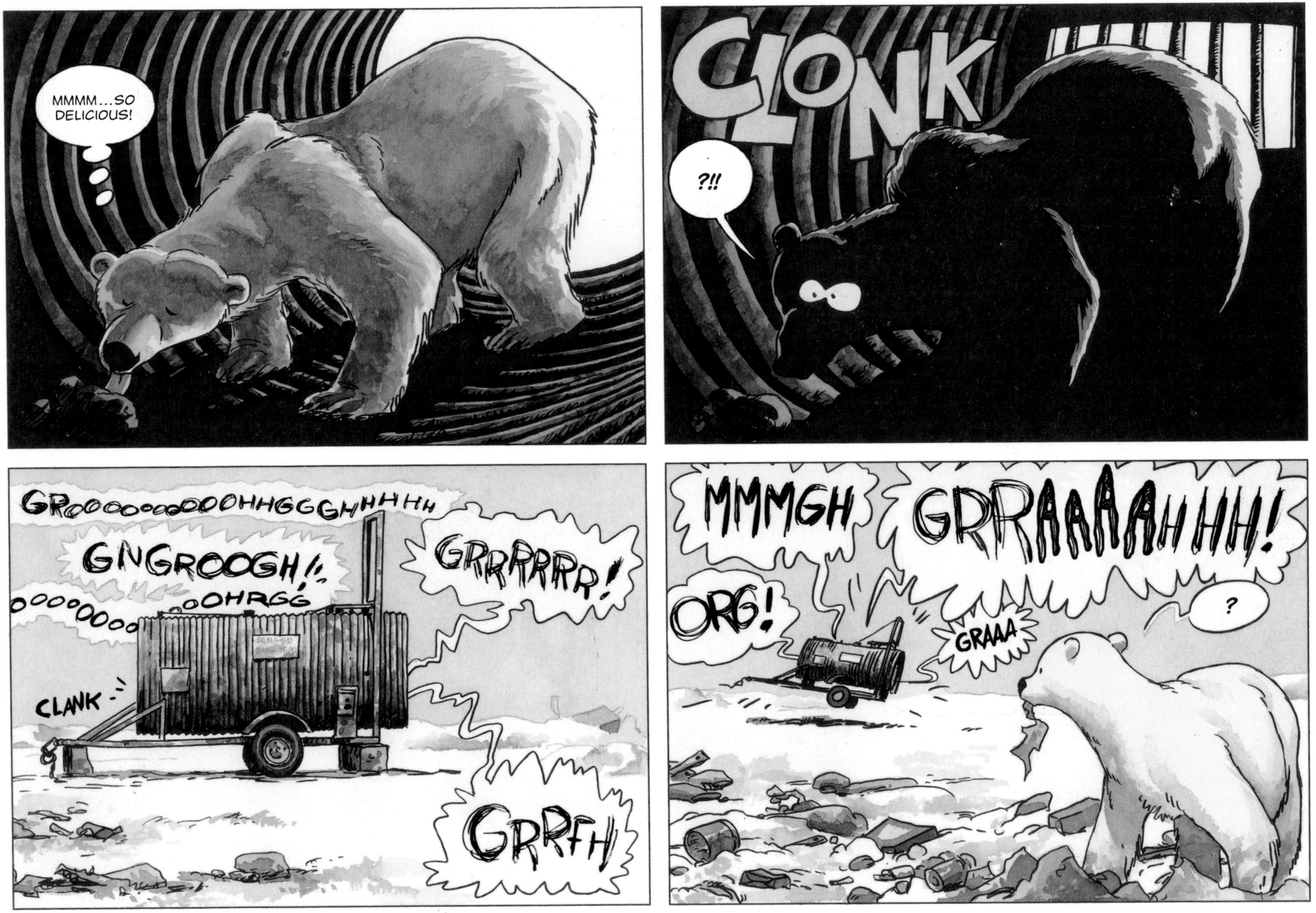
MMMM...SO DELICIOUS!
CLONK
?!!
GROOOOOOOOOOOHHGGGHHHHH
GNGROOGH!
GRRRRRRR!
OOOOOOOOO OOHRGG
CLANK
GRRFH
MMMGH
GRRAAAAAHHHH!
ORG!
GRAAA
?

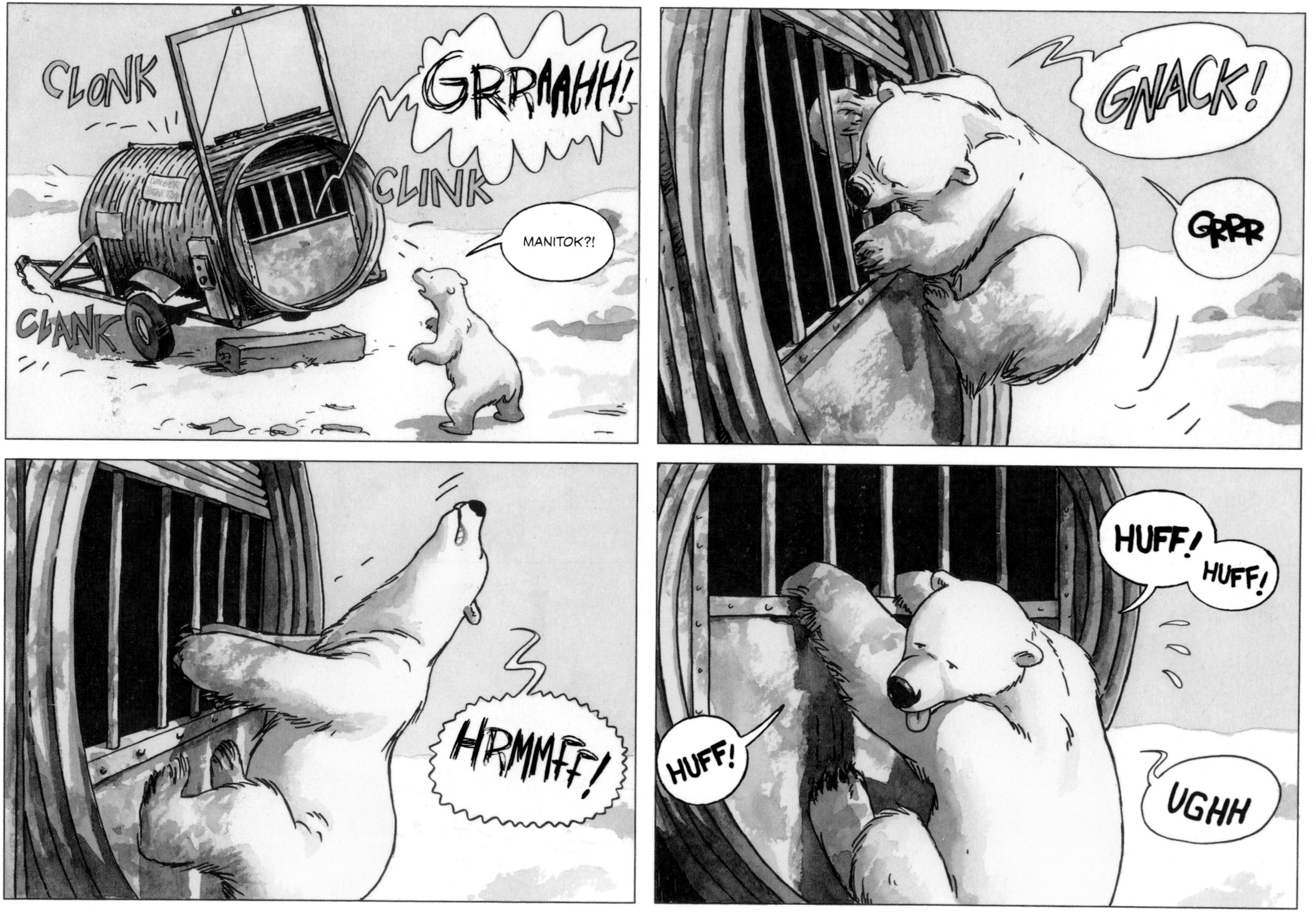
CLONK
GRRAAHH!
CLINK
CLANK
MANITOK?!
GNACK!
GRRR
HRMMFF!
HUFF!
HUFF!
HUFF!
UGHH

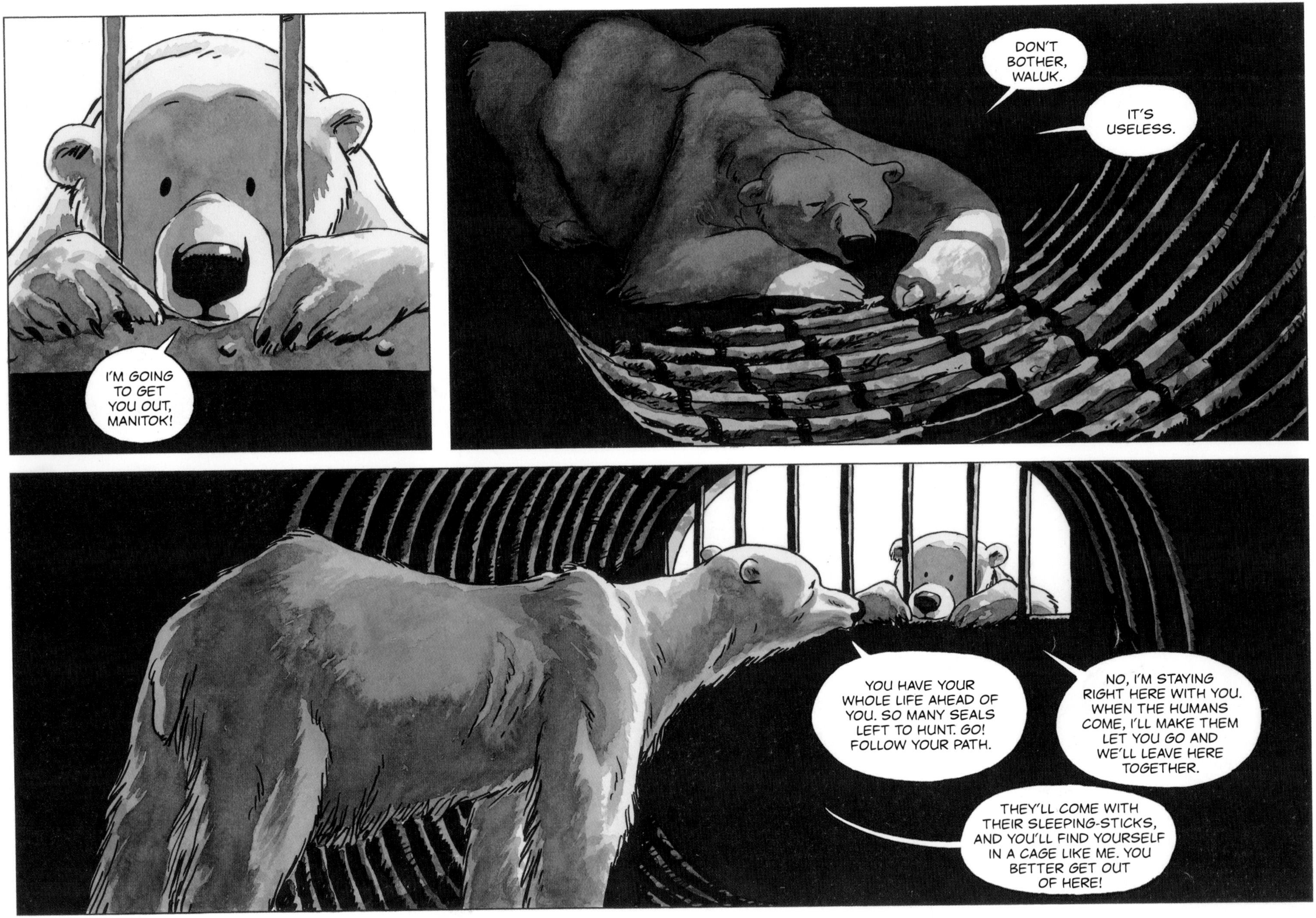
I'M GOING TO GET YOU OUT, MANITOK!
DON'T BOTHER, WALUK.
IT'S USELESS.
YOU HAVE YOUR WHOLE LIFE AHEAD OF YOU. SO MANY SEALS LEFT TO HUNT. GO! FOLLOW YOUR PATH.
NO, I'M STAYING RIGHT HERE WITH YOU. WHEN THE HUMANS COME, I'LL MAKE THEM LET YOU GO AND WE'LL LEAVE HERE TOGETHER.
THEY'LL COME WITH THEIR SLEEPING-STICKS, AND YOU'LL FIND YOURSELF IN A CAGE LIKE ME. YOU BETTER GET OUT OF HERE!

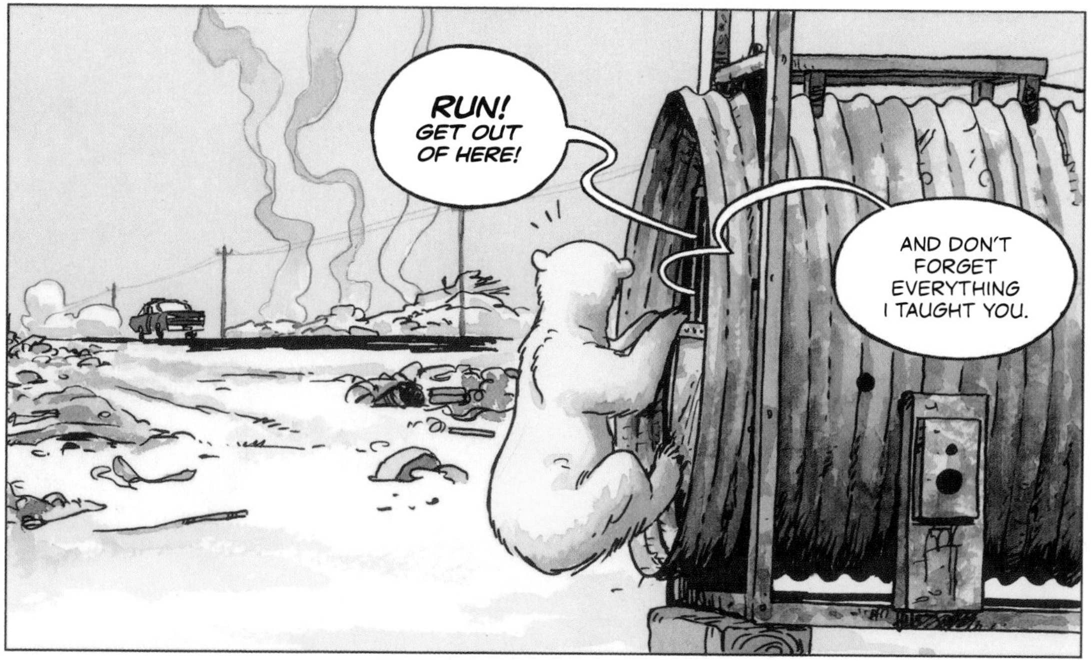
RUN! GET OUT OF HERE!
AND DON'T FORGET EVERYTHING I TAUGHT YOU.

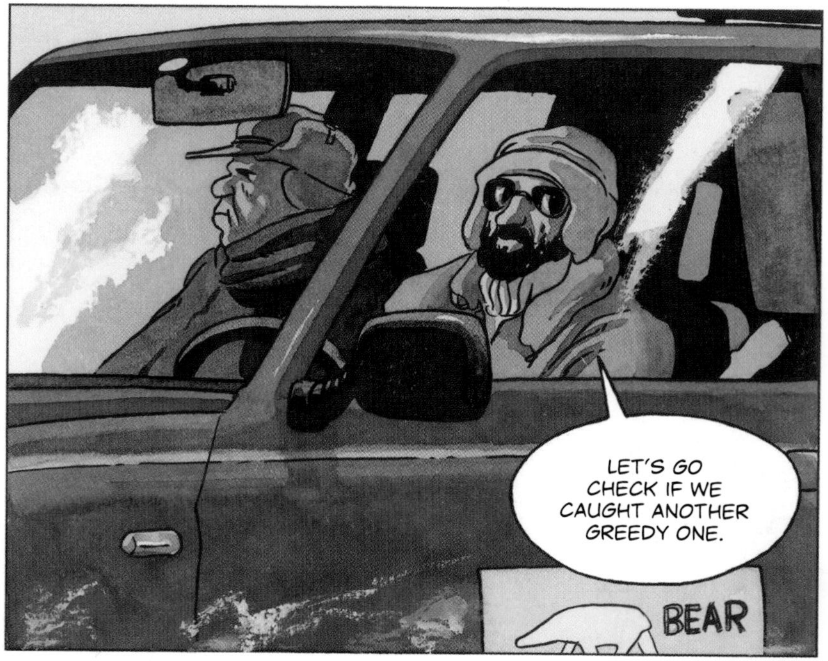
LET'S GO CHECK IF WE CAUGHT ANOTHER GREEDY ONE.
BEAR

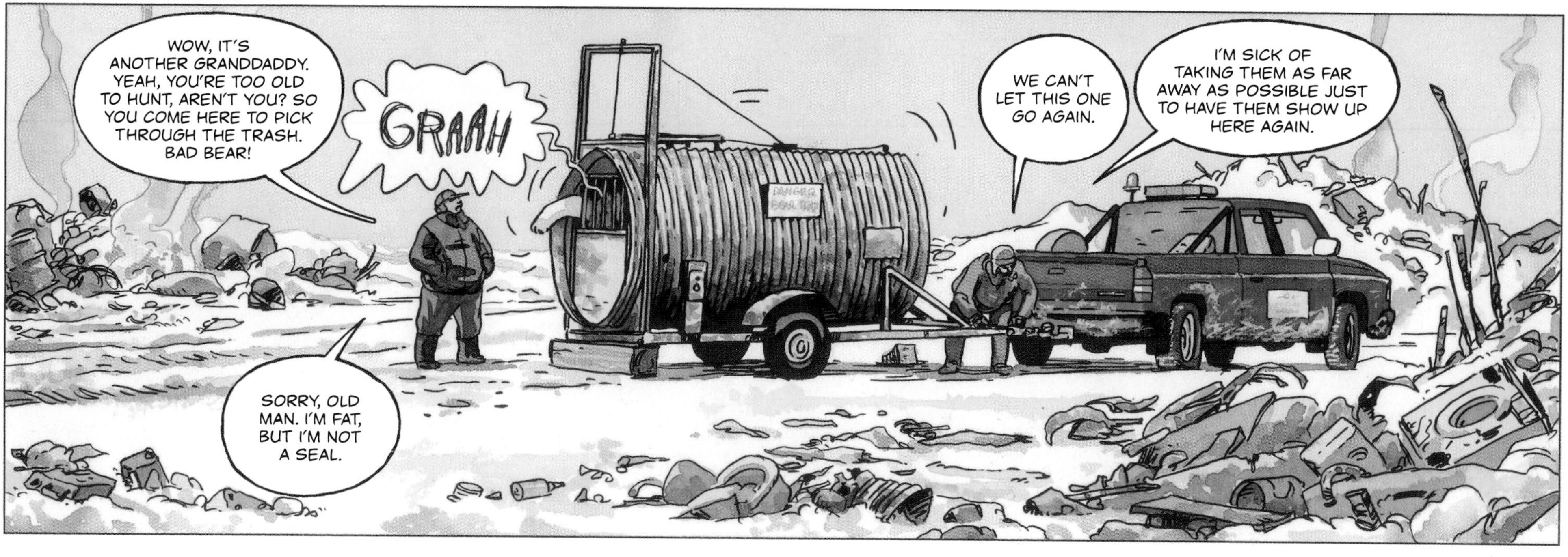
WOW, IT'S ANOTHER GRANDDADDY. YEAH, YOU'RE TOO OLD TO HUNT, AREN'T YOU? SO YOU COME HERE TO PICK THROUGH THE TRASH. BAD BEAR!
GRAAH
SORRY, OLD MAN. I'M FAT, BUT I'M NOT A SEAL.
WE CAN'T LET THIS ONE GO AGAIN.
I'M SICK OF TAKING THEM AS FAR AWAY AS POSSIBLE JUST TO HAVE THEM SHOW UP HERE AGAIN.

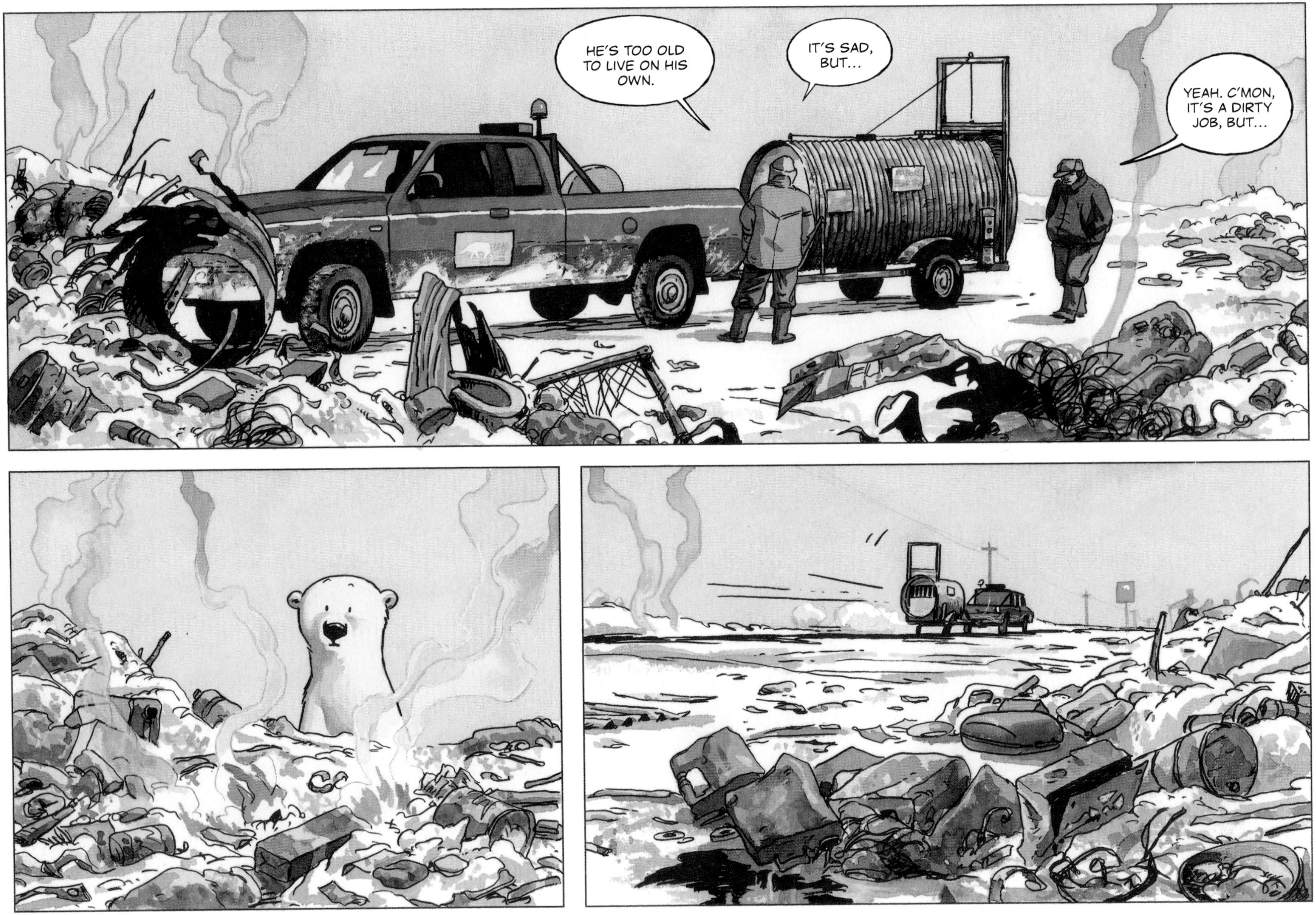
HE'S TOO OLD TO LIVE ON HIS OWN.
IT'S SAD, BUT...
YEAH. C'MON, IT'S A DIRTY JOB, BUT...

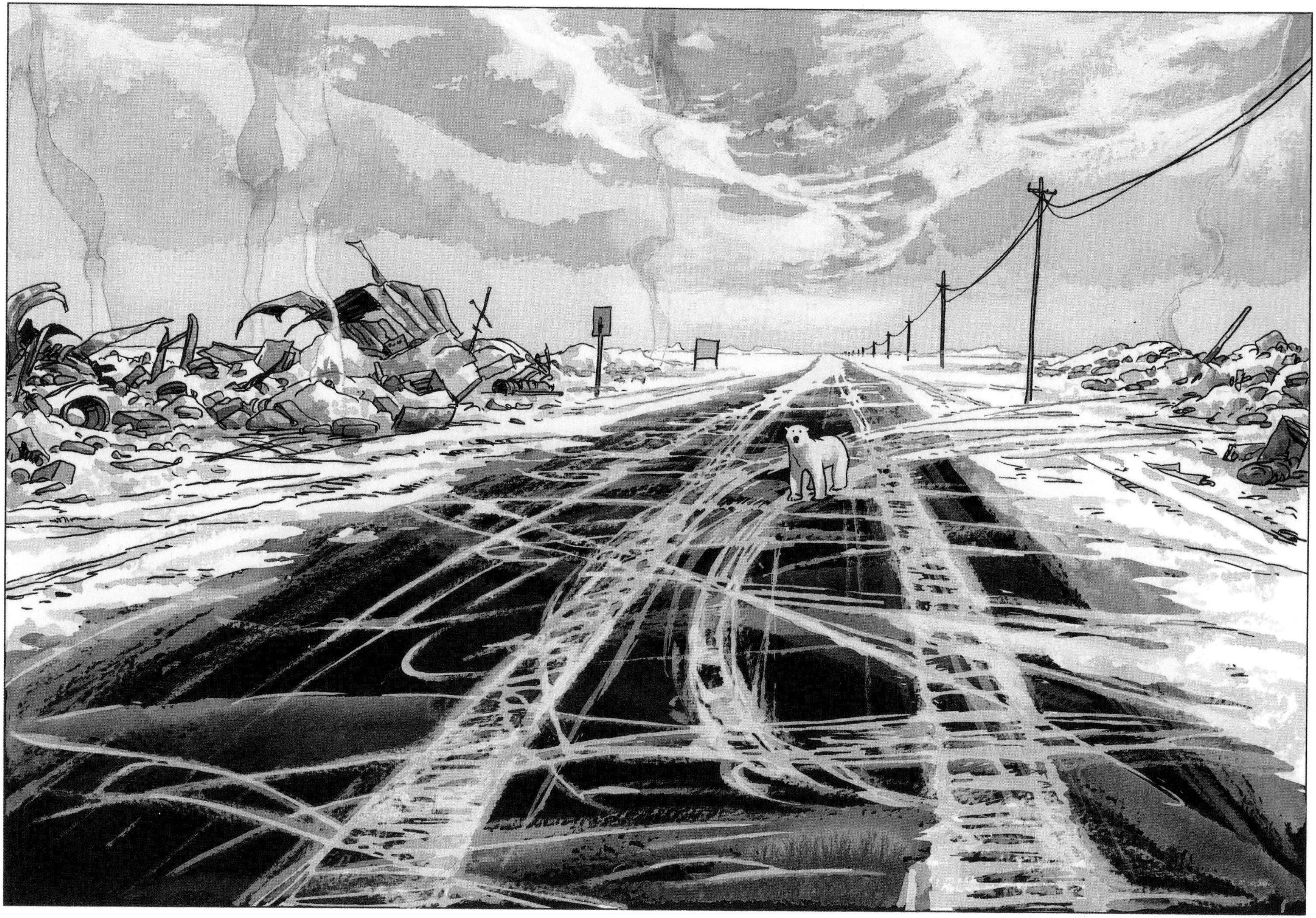

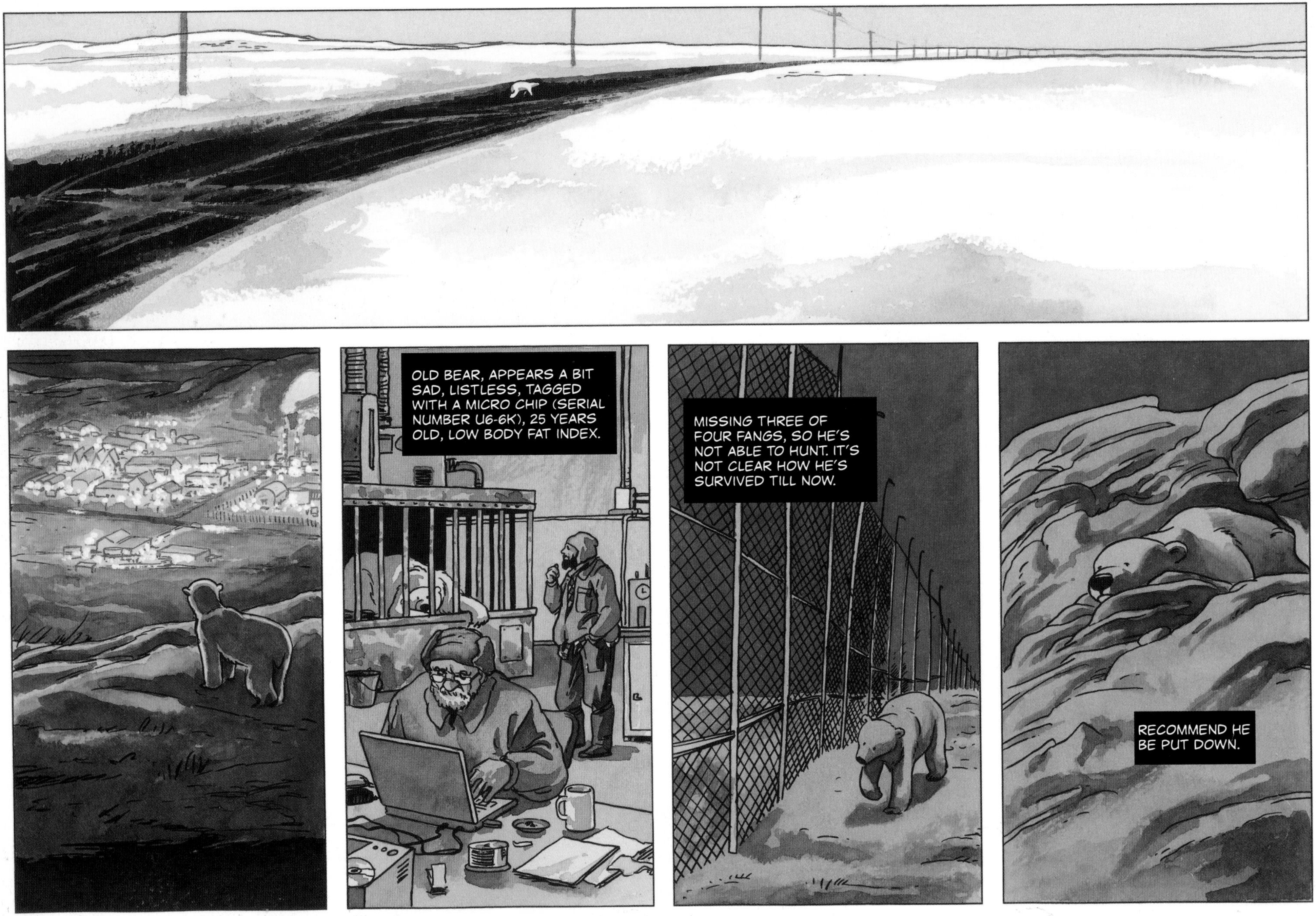
OLD BEAR, APPEARS A BIT SAD, LISTLESS, TAGGED WITH A MICRO CHIP (SERIAL NUMBER U6-6K), 25 YEARS OLD, LOW BODY FAT INDEX.
MISSING THREE OF FOUR FANGS, SO HE'S NOT ABLE TO HUNT. IT'S NOT CLEAR HOW HE'S SURVIVED TILL NOW.
RECOMMEND HE BE PUT DOWN.

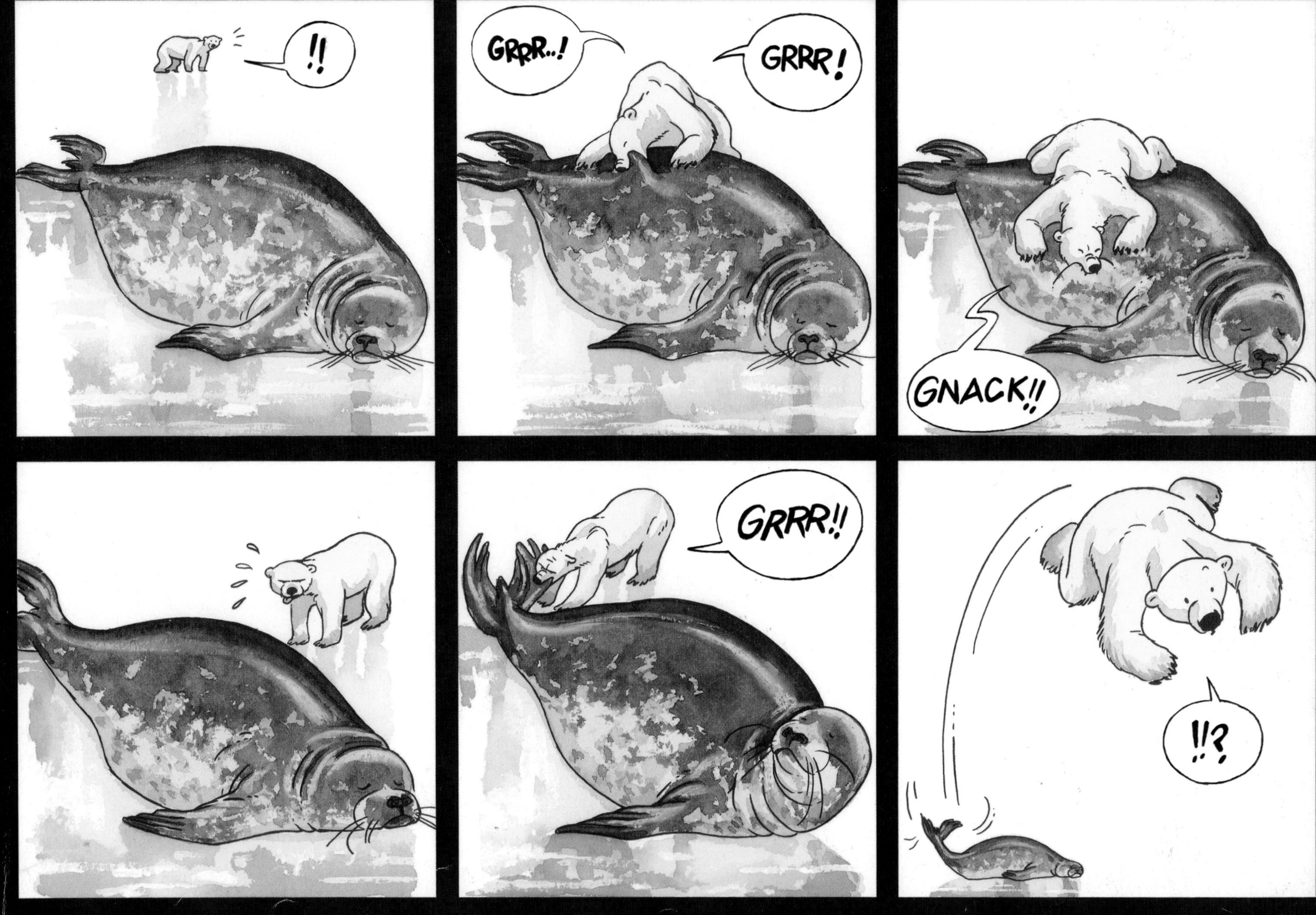
!!
GRRR..!
GRRR!
GNACK!!
GRRR!!
!!?

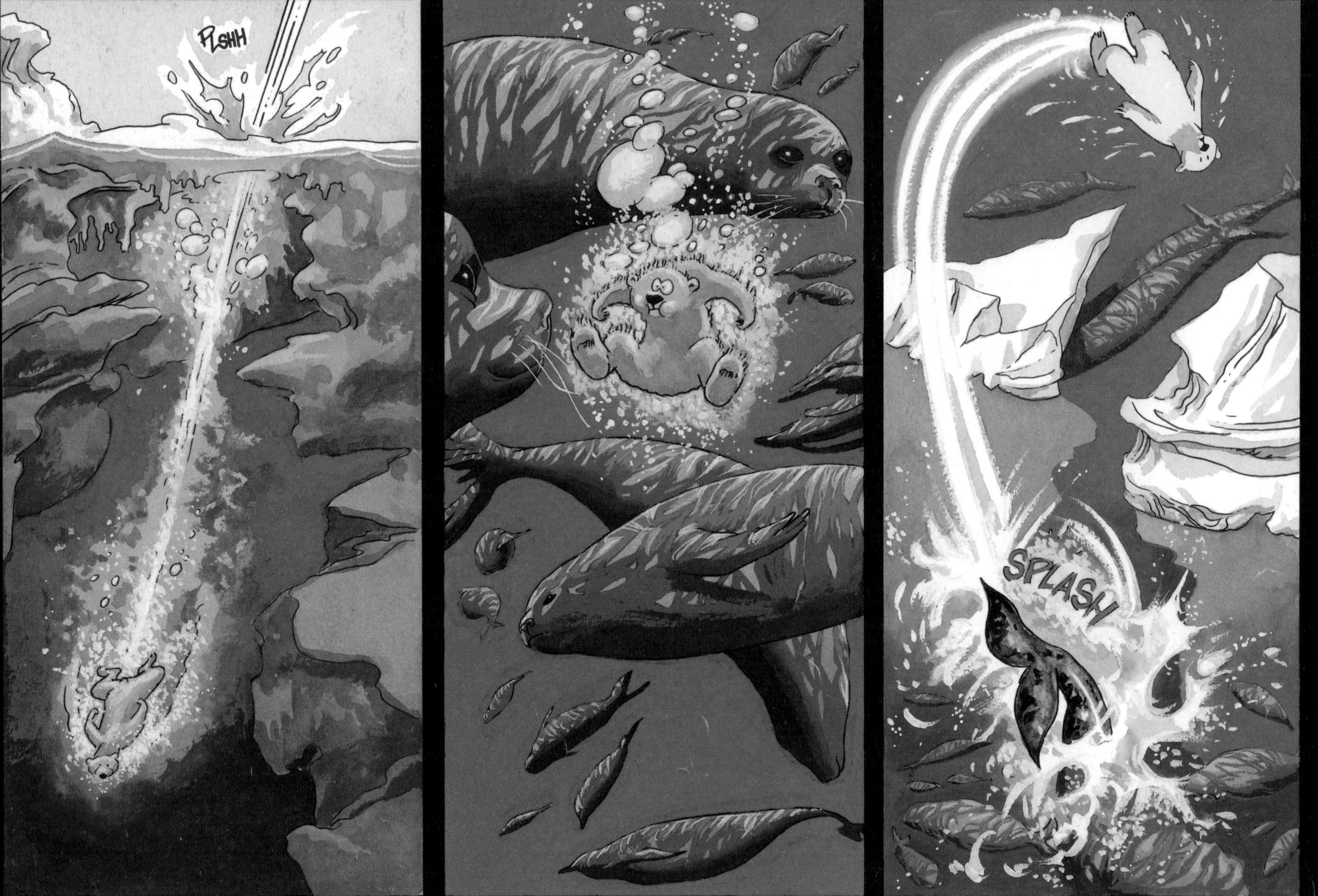
PLSHH
SPLASH

AH!

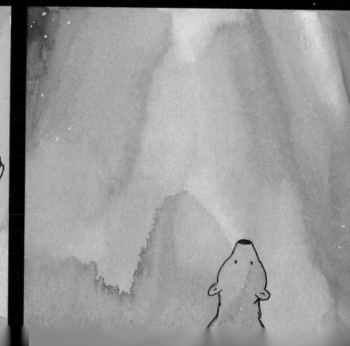

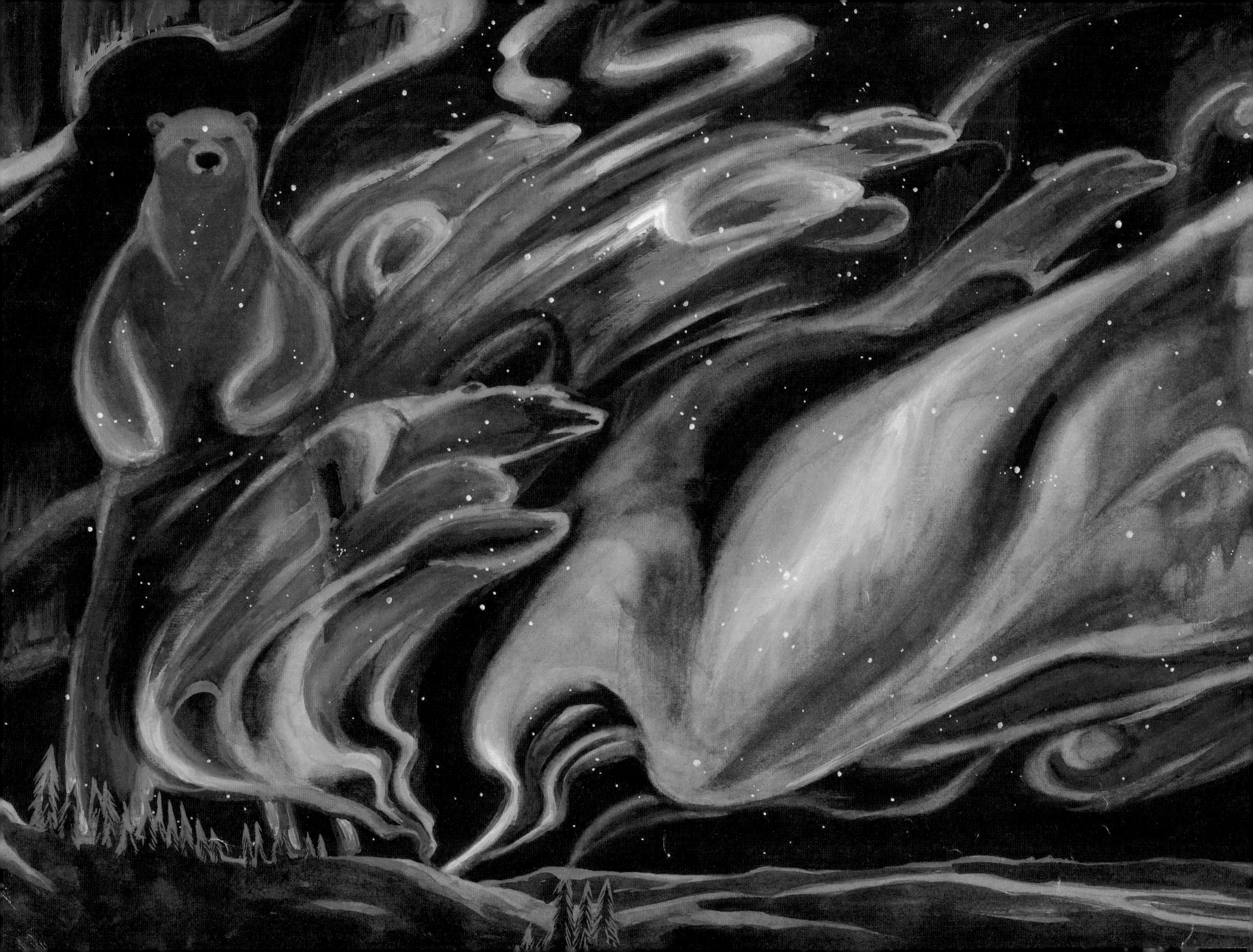

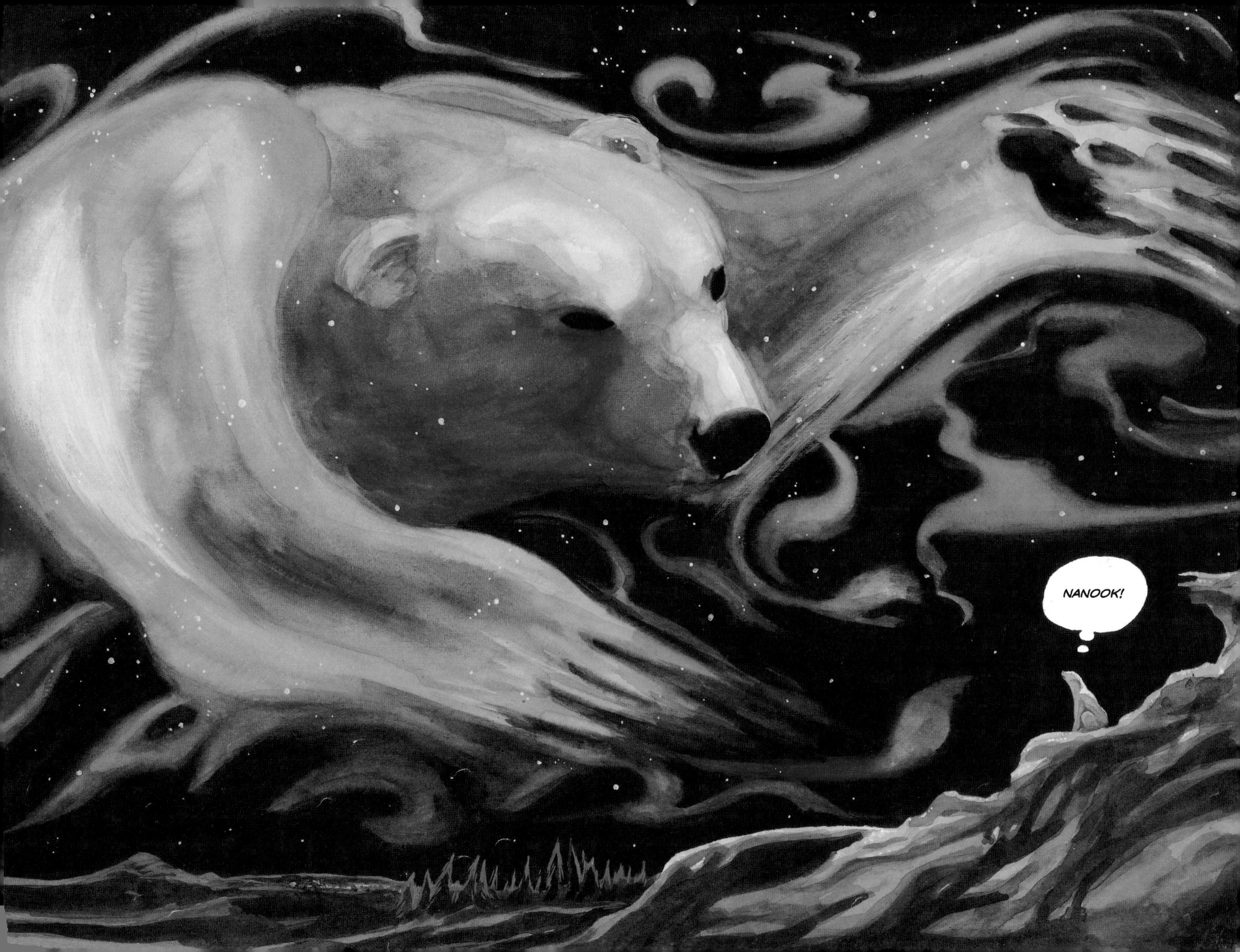
NANOOK!

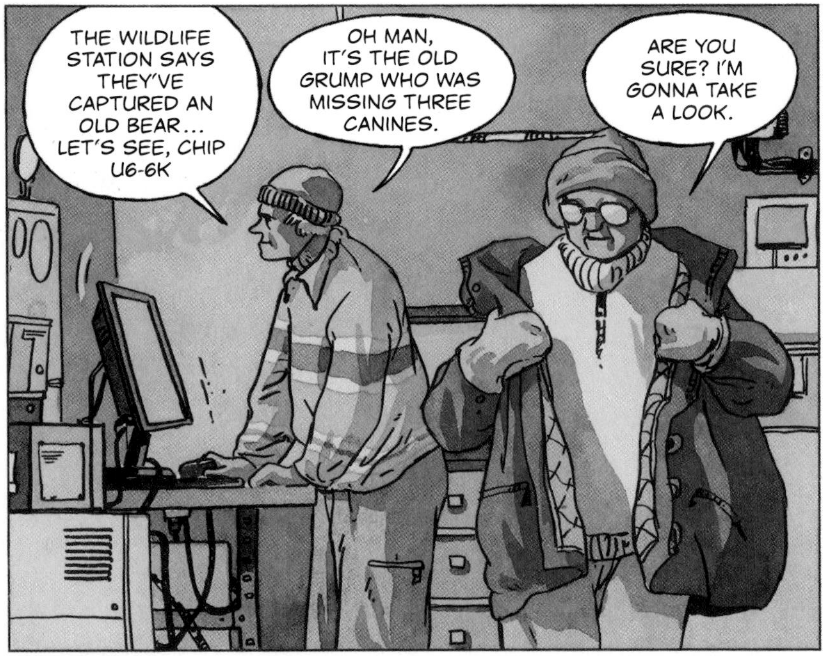
THE WILDLIFE STATION SAYS THEY'VE CAPTURED AN OLD BEAR... LET'S SEE, CHIP U6-6K
OH MAN, IT'S THE OLD GRUMP WHO WAS MISSING THREE CANINES.
ARE YOU SURE? I'M GONNA TAKE A LOOK.

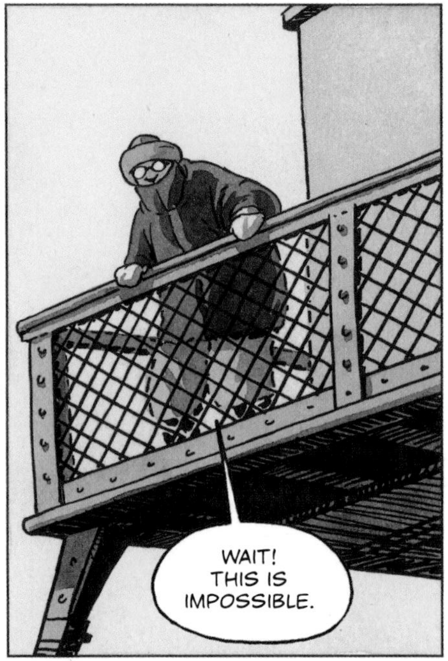
WAIT! THIS IS IMPOSSIBLE.

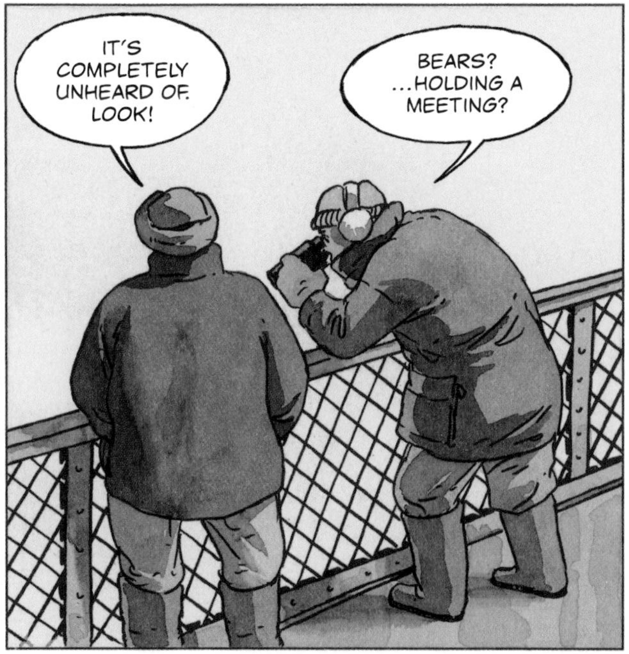
IT'S COMPLETELY UNHEARD OF. LOOK!
BEARS? ...HOLDING A MEETING?

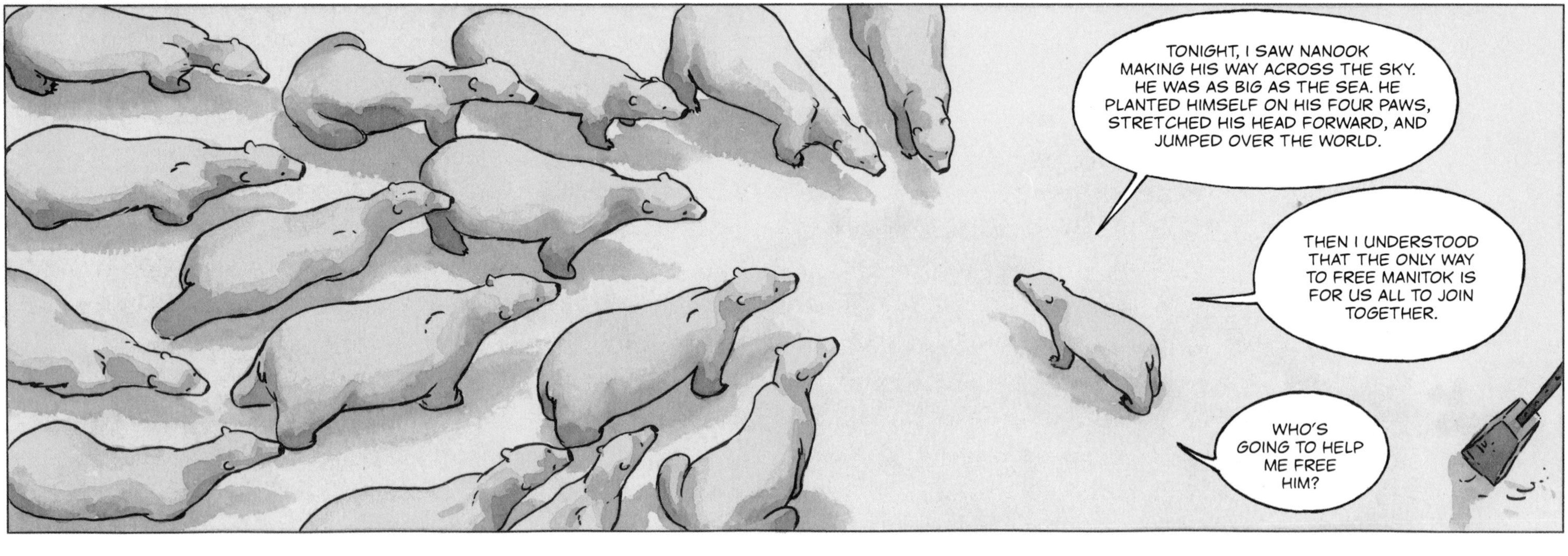
TONIGHT, I SAW NANOOK MAKING HIS WAY ACROSS THE SKY. HE WAS AS BIG AS THE SEA. HE PLANTED HIMSELF ON HIS FOUR PAWS, STRETCHED HIS HEAD FORWARD, AND JUMPED OVER THE WORLD.
THEN I UNDERSTOOD THAT THE ONLY WAY TO FREE MANITOK IS FOR US ALL TO JOIN TOGETHER.
WHO'S GOING TO HELP ME FREE HIM?

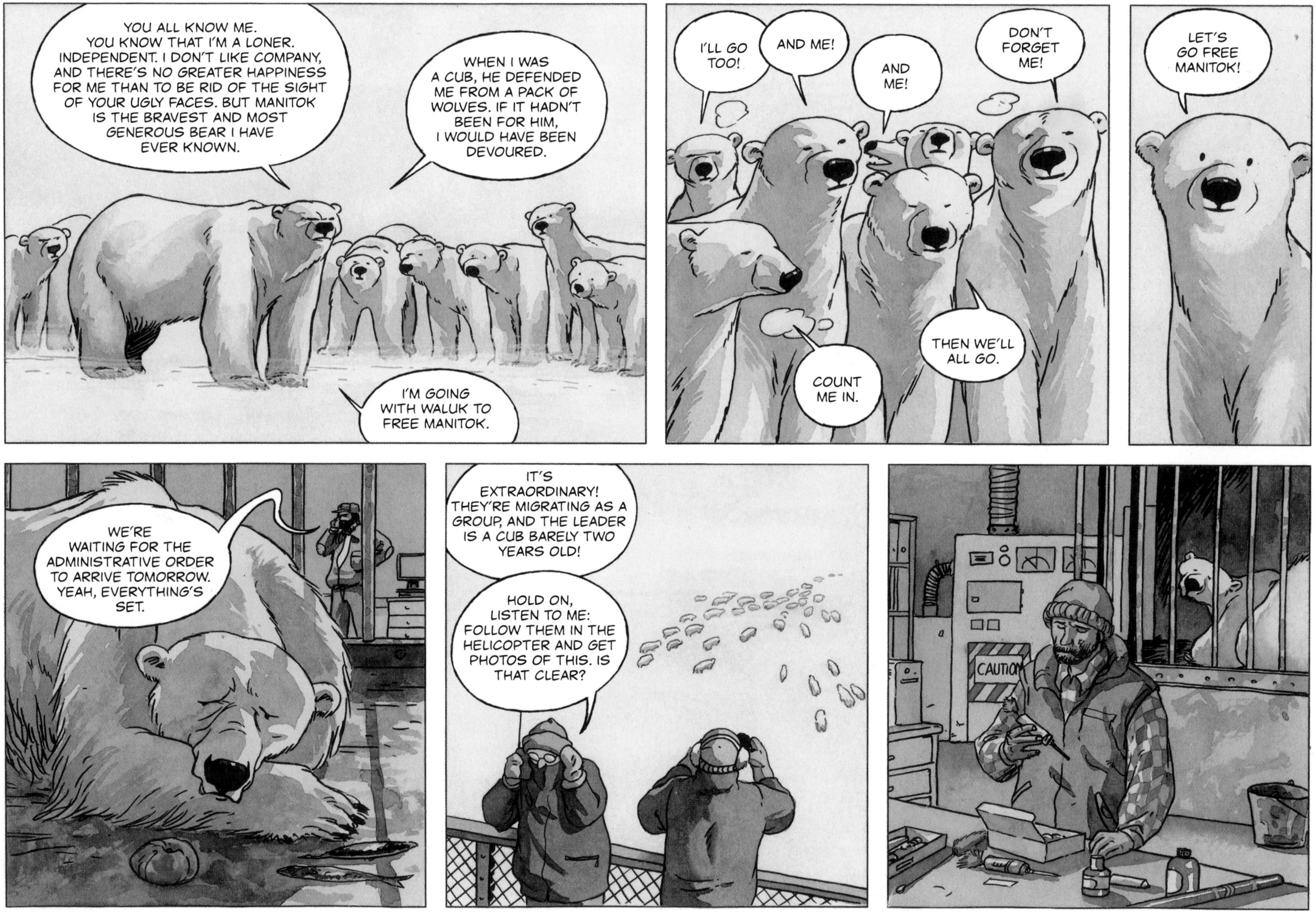
YOU ALL KNOW ME. YOU KNOW THAT I'M A LONER. INDEPENDENT. I DON'T LIKE COMPANY, AND THERE'S NO GREATER HAPPINESS FOR ME THAN TO BE RID OF THE SIGHT OF YOUR UGLY FACES. BUT MANITOK IS THE BRAVEST AND MOST GENEROUS BEAR I HAVE EVER KNOWN.
WHEN I WAS A CUB, HE DEFENDED ME FROM A PACK OF WOLVES. IF IT HADN'T BEEN FOR HIM, I WOULD HAVE BEEN DEVOURED.
I'M GOING WITH WALUK TO FREE MANITOK.
I'LL GO TOO!
AND ME!
AND ME!
DON'T FORGET ME!
COUNT ME IN.
THEN WE'LL ALL GO.
LET'S GO FREE MANITOK!
WE'RE WAITING FOR THE ADMINISTRATIVE ORDER TO ARRIVE TOMORROW. YEAH, EVERYTHING'S SET.
IT'S EXTRAORDINARY! THEY'RE MIGRATING AS A GROUP, AND THE LEADER IS A CUB BARELY TWO YEARS OLD!
HOLD ON, LISTEN TO ME: FOLLOW THEM IN THE HELICOPTER AND GET PHOTOS OF THIS. IS THAT CLEAR?
CAUTION

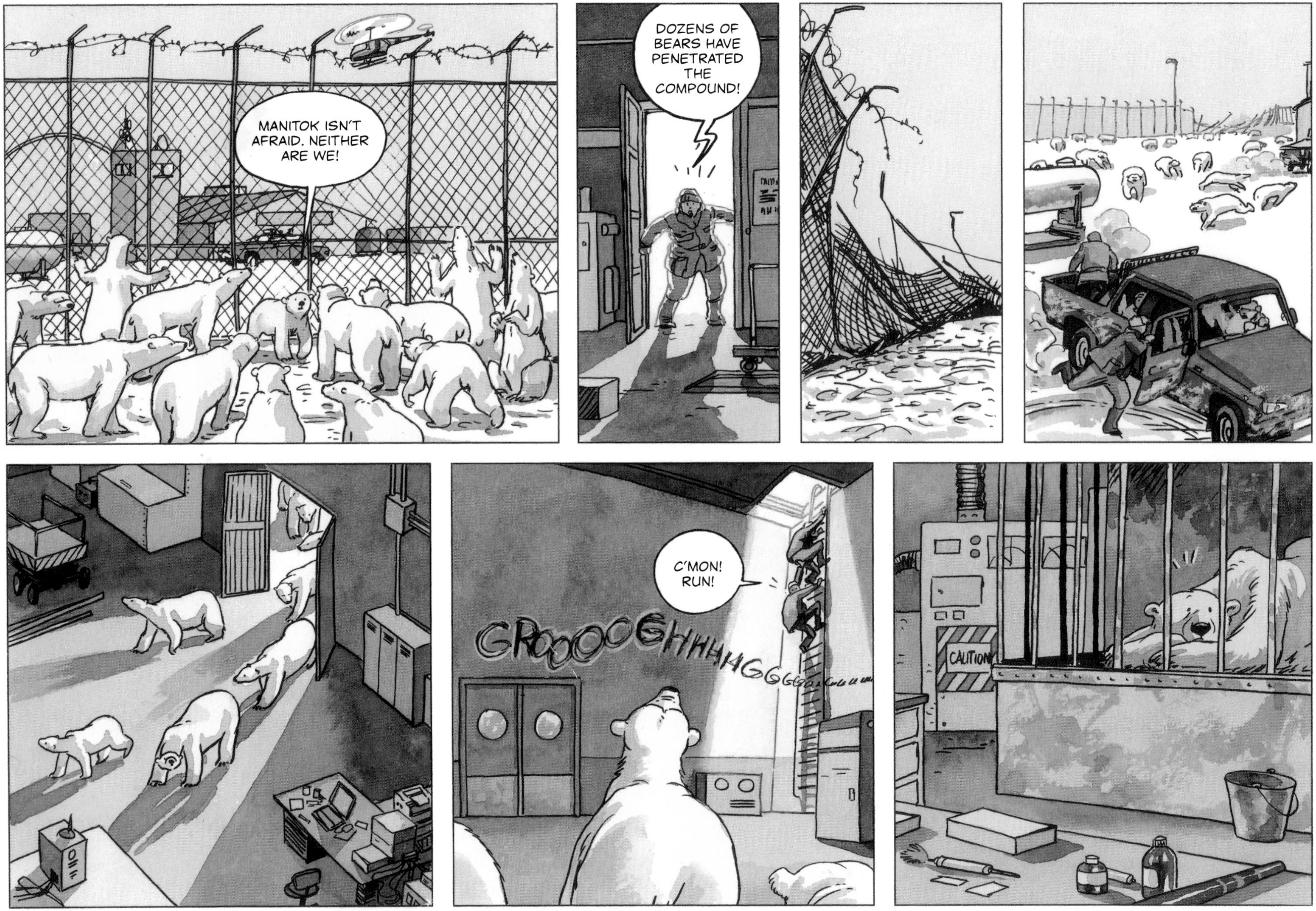
MANITOK ISN'T AFRAID. NEITHER ARE WE!
DOZENS OF BEARS HAVE PENETRATED THE COMPOUND!
C'MON! RUN!
GROOOOGHHHHGGG
CAUTION

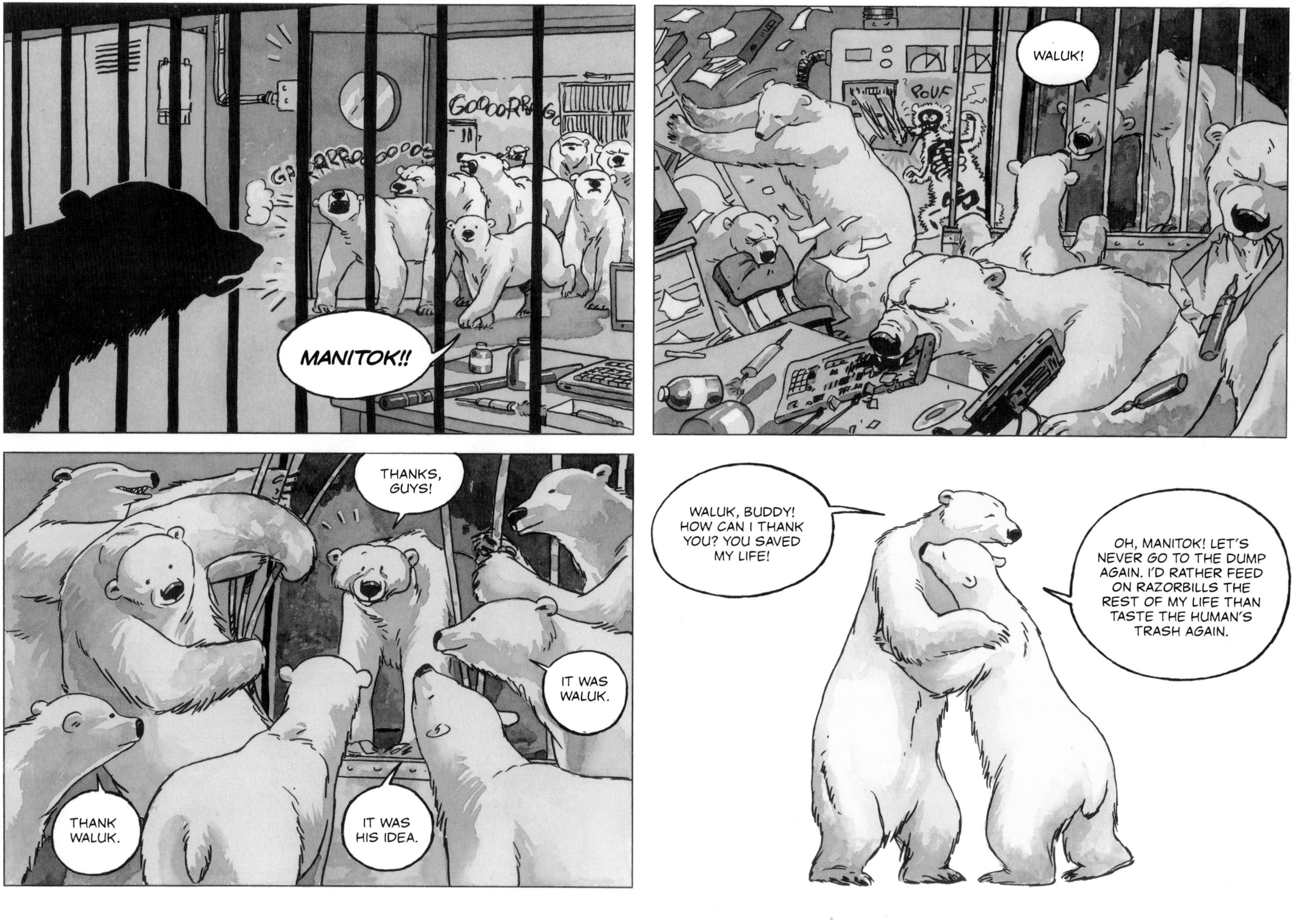
MANITOK!!
WALUK!
POUF
THANKS, GUYS!
IT WAS WALUK.
THANK WALUK.
IT WAS HIS IDEA.
WALUK, BUDDY! HOW CAN I THANK YOU? YOU SAVED MY LIFE!
OH, MANITOK! LET'S NEVER GO TO THE DUMP AGAIN. I'D RATHER FEED ON RAZORBILLS THE REST OF MY LIFE THAN TASTE THE HUMAN'S TRASH AGAIN.

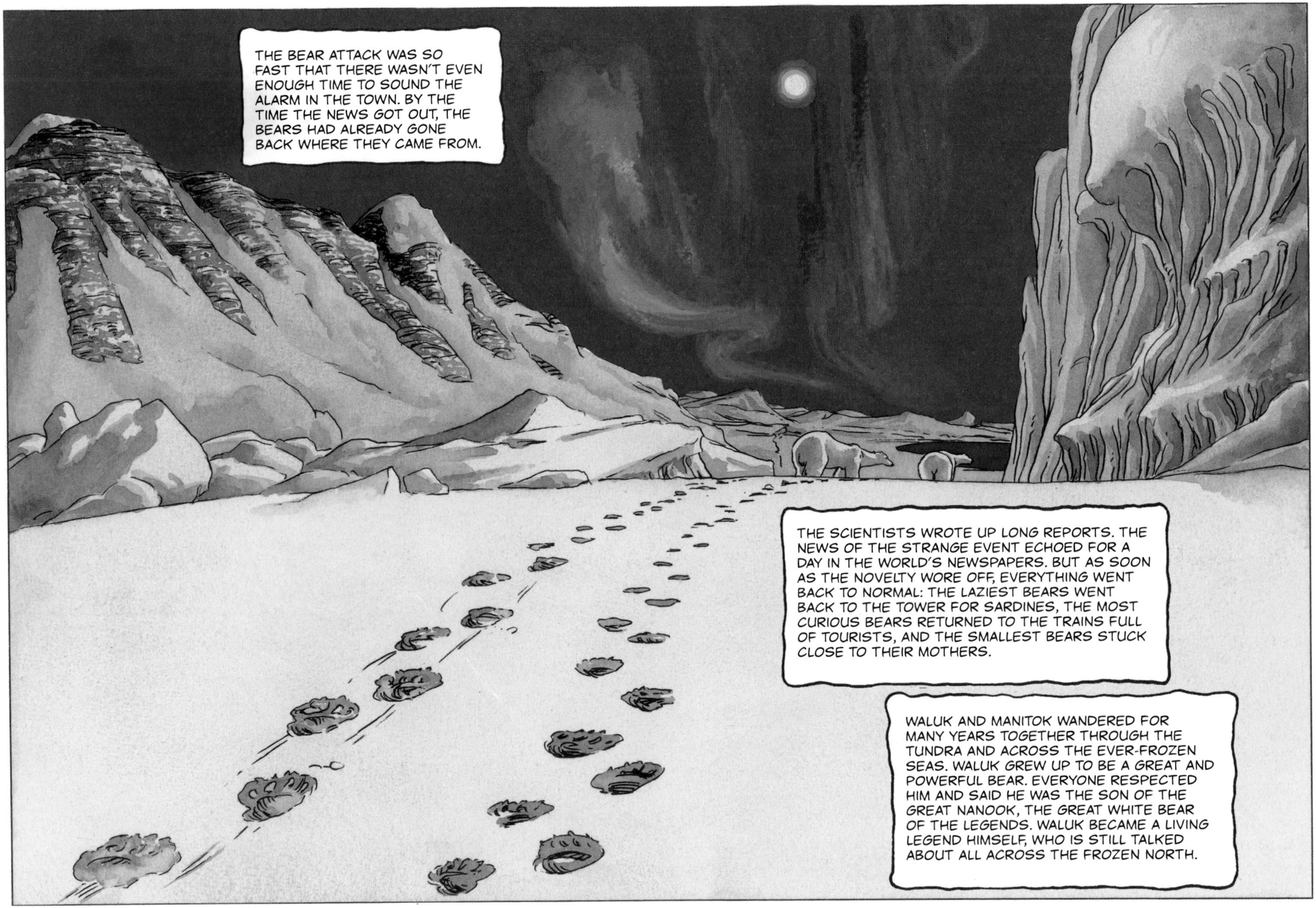
THE BEAR ATTACK WAS SO FAST THAT THERE WASN'T EVEN ENOUGH TIME TO SOUND THE ALARM IN THE TOWN. BY THE TIME THE NEWS GOT OUT, THE BEARS HAD ALREADY GONE BACK WHERE THEY CAME FROM.
THE SCIENTISTS WROTE UP LONG REPORTS. THE NEWS OF THE STRANGE EVENT ECHOED FOR A DAY IN THE WORLD'S NEWSPAPERS. BUT AS SOON AS THE NOVELTY WORE OFF, EVERYTHING WENT BACK TO NORMAL: THE LAZIEST BEARS WENT BACK TO THE TOWER FOR SARDINES, THE MOST CURIOUS BEARS RETURNED TO THE TRAINS FULL OF TOURISTS, AND THE SMALLEST BEARS STUCK CLOSE TO THEIR MOTHERS.
WALUK AND MANITOK WANDERED FOR MANY YEARS TOGETHER THROUGH THE TUNDRA AND ACROSS THE EVER-FROZEN SEAS. WALUK GREW UP TO BE A GREAT AND POWERFUL BEAR. EVERYONE RESPECTED HIM AND SAID HE WAS THE SON OF THE GREAT NANOOK, THE GREAT WHITE BEAR OF THE LEGENDS. WALUK BECAME A LIVING LEGEND HIMSELF, WHO IS STILL TALKED ABOUT ALL ACROSS THE FROZEN NORTH.

ARE POLAR BEARS IN DANGER?

With endless ice and temperatures as cold as –50 degrees Fahrenheit (–46° C), the Arctic would be too harsh for most animals, but it is perfect for the polar bear. Polar bears are adapted for the cold. Not only do they have their characteristic heavy white fur for insulation, but the skin beneath is thick and black, which helps absorb heat from the sun. And underneath the skin, polar bears have a layer of stored fat called blubber. Blubber can be up to four inches (10 centimeters) thick, providing even more warmth.

The polar bear is a marine mammal, meaning it depends on the sea for both food and habitat. The animal they hunt most is the ringed seal, which lives in the Arctic Ocean. Ringed seals swim under the sea ice to hunt for their own food. The seals create holes in the ice so that they can come up for air. Polar bears see the holes and wait above. When a polar bear spots a seal coming up for a breath, it pounces on the seal, digging its teeth into the seal's head.

The meal that soon follows is an important part of a polar bear's diet because it is rich in fat. While polar bears rely on seals for most of their diet, other sources of food include walruses, dead whales that wash up onshore, birds, bird eggs, and some vegetation.

Polar bears spend much of their lives on sea ice, creating dens to nurse their young. Many float on sea ice and move from one place to another to find food or mates.

If the Arctic is perfect for such an animal, then why are polar bears like Waluk and Manitok in danger? One threat to polar bears is global warming. Global warming is the result of humans using fossil fuels such as oil, gas, and coal. Fossil fuels trap heat and light from the sun in Earth's atmosphere, which makes the planet warmer. As the temperature of Earth increases, Arctic sea ice melts. With less sea ice, polar bears can't hunt seals as easily. This means bears struggle to find food and that they are less healthy.

The disappearing sea ice also means that polar bears have to migrate farther to hunt, mate, and make dens. This longer migration can also make them weaker. Many polar bears, like Waluk and Manitok, are forced to eat less nourishing foods like birds' eggs and vegetation because they cannot hunt seals.

Some scientists have studied female polar bears' nutrition and their ability to give birth to healthy cubs. These scientists have noticed that female polar bears with low body fat will not get pregnant until they put on more fat. Those female polar bears that do get pregnant often struggle to find enough food to sustain themselves and their cubs. Because there is less food, the cubs are weaker and less able to survive on their own (like Waluk). Many polar bear cubs don't survive after their mothers leave them because they cannot find enough food.

As the Arctic sea ice melts, the polar bear population is at risk. Scientists think today's polar bear population is between 20,000 and 25,000 bears. They fear that by the year 2050, there could be as few as 6,700 to 8,400 polar bears left in the wild.

While global warming is the main threat to the polar bear population, it is not the only threat. Another major threat is oil and gas drilling. Oil companies are interested in the Arctic region because of the oil and gas buried beneath the ocean. Drilling for this oil can be very harmful to the habitats of polar bears and other Arctic wildlife.

Another threat to polar bears is contact with humans. As the climate has warmed, polar bears have traveled farther to find food. This has caused encounters between humans and polar bears to increase. Such encounters rarely end well for the bears.

The good news is that polar bears were listed as a threatened species on the United States Endangered Species Act in 2008. There are many organizations that are working to protect polar bears and the Arctic region. Check out these websites to learn how you can help!

National Wildlife Federation
http://www.nwf.org/Wildlife/Threats-to-Wildlife/Global-Warming/Effects-on-Wildlife-and-Habitat/Polar-Bears.aspx

Polar Bears International
http://www.polarbearsinternational.org/

World Wildlife Fund
http://worldwildlife.org/species/polar-bear

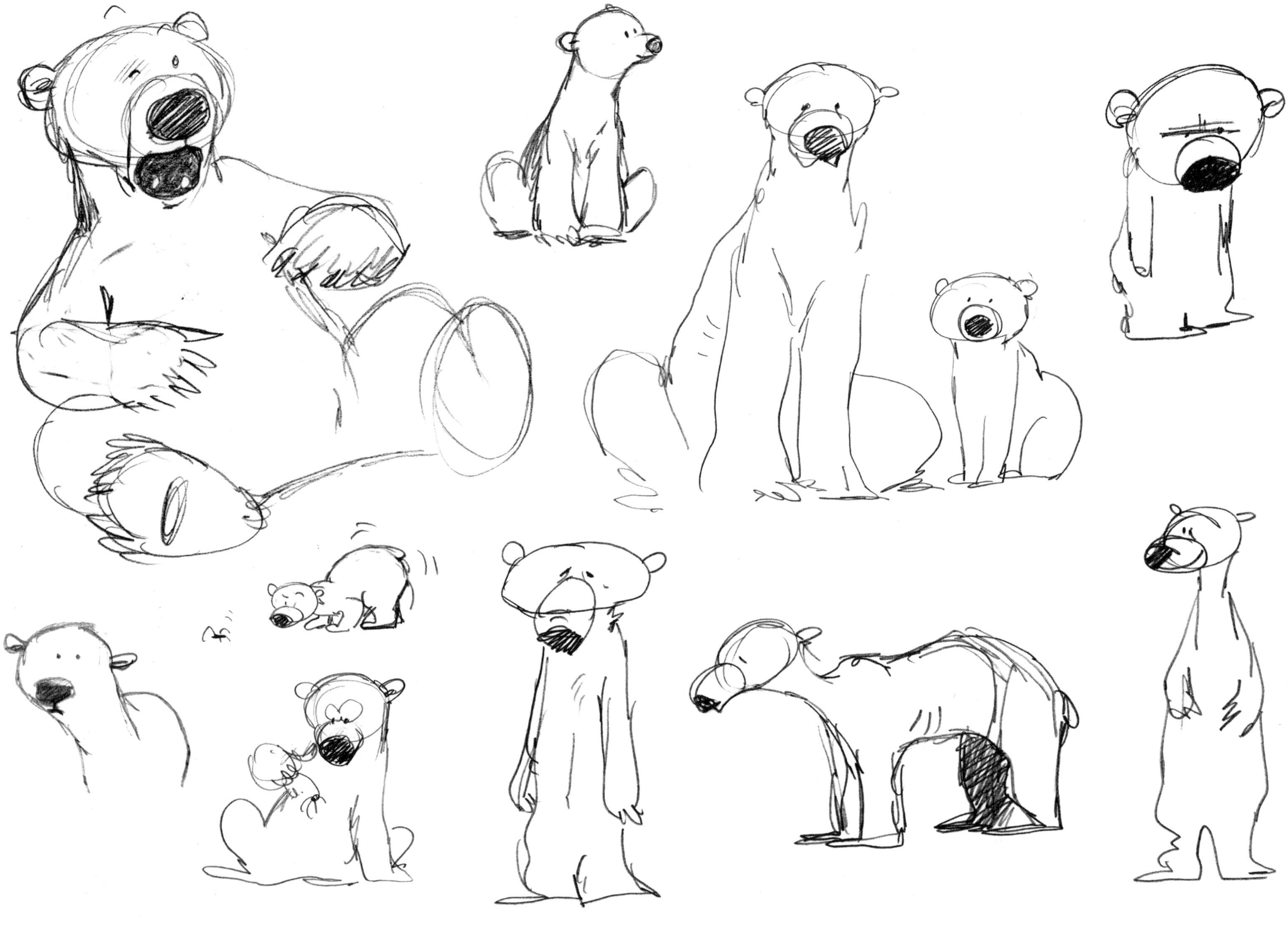

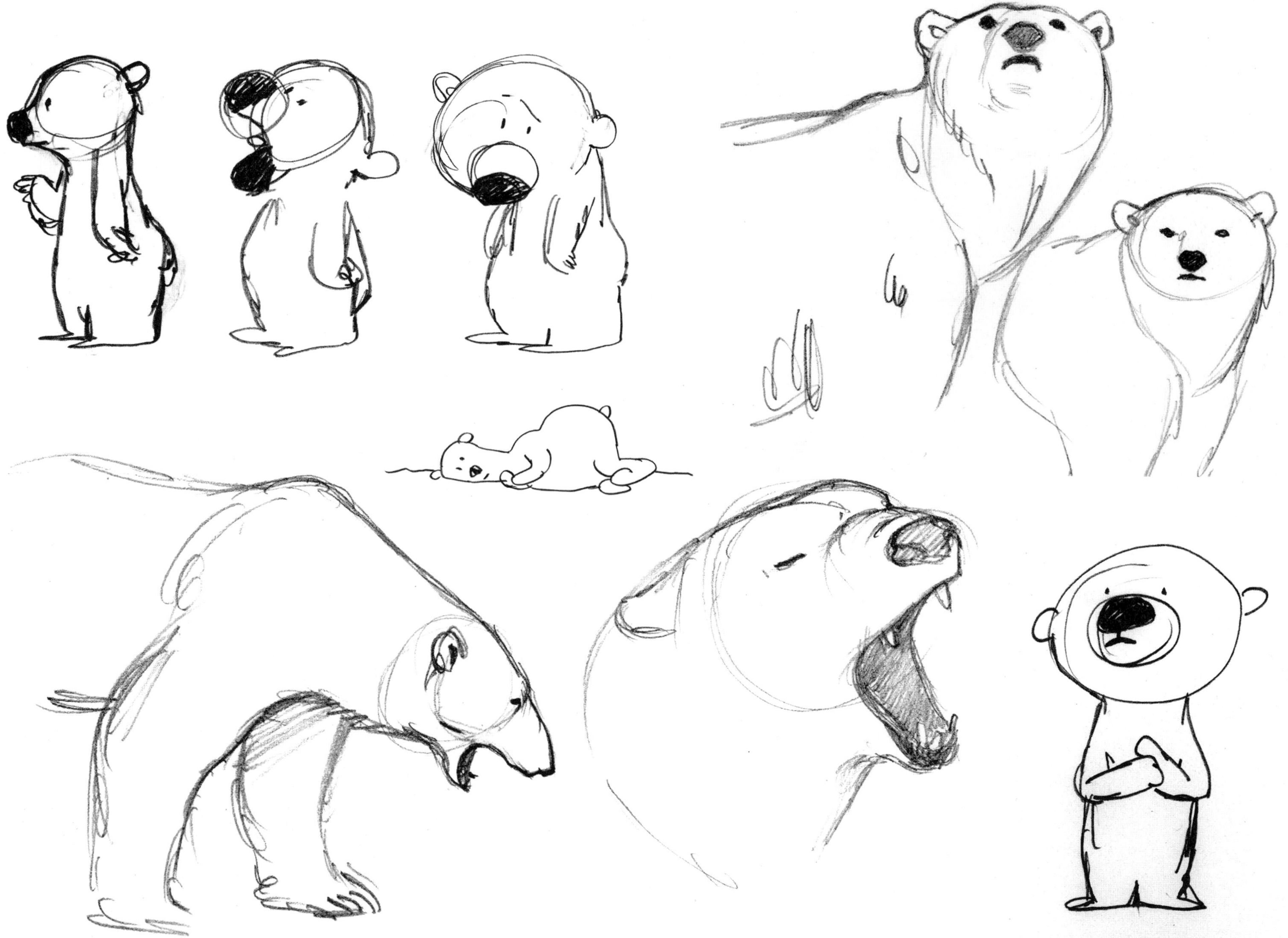

ABOUT THE AUTHOR AND THE ILLUSTRATOR

EMILIO RUIZ was born in Spain in 1960, received a bachelor of fine arts from the Polytechnic University of Valencia, and began a career as a photographer in 1982. He started in the world of advertising, then moved on to designing scenery for theater and dance productions and to work as a designer on a documentary series. He has collaborated with Ana Miralles on several graphic novels: the trilogy En busca del unicornio (Glénat, 1996–1999), and *De mano en mano* (De Ponent, 2009). Ana Miralles and Emilio Ruiz are currently working together on the four-part series Muraqqa, the story of a woman artist in the court of the Mughal king Jahangir in the early seventeenth century.

ANA MIRALLES, born in Madrid in 1959, has been a professional comics and magazine illustrator since 1982. Her work has been published in prominent periodicals, including *Marie-Claire* and *Vogue*, and in a broad array of children's books, posters, book covers, albums, and advertising. She has also worked in the theater and the cinema as a costume designer, a backdrop artist, and a storyboarder. She has illustrated graphic novels for both the Spanish and French markets, including several collaborations with Emilio Ruiz, eleven volumes in the Djinn series (Dargaud Benelux) and adaptations of literary classics into comics for French magazine *Je Bouquine*. She received the Grand Prize of the Salón de Barcelona 2009 in recognition of her long career in the world of comics.